His lip ....g **tingles all the way to her toes.**

Her body was instantly on fire, her tongue reluctantly anticipating the silky feel of his. "This doesn't solve our problems."

"No," he answered, then used his tongue to stroke fire into her mouth, pulling out the moment she was about to give in. "But it's a damn good start to our reconciliation."

He wasn't lying about that, Felicia thought, and then leaned her body against his. His arms wrapped quickly around her, locking her in place. "You're not playing fair," she gasped, then nibbled on his bottom lip, loving the brush of his low-trimmed goatee against her face.

"All's fair in love and war."

Books by A.C. Arthur

Kimani Romance

Love Me Like No Other
A Cinderella Affair
Guarding His Body
Second Chance, Baby

A.C. ARTHUR

was born and raised in Baltimore, Maryland, where she currently resides with her husband and three children. An active imagination and a love for reading encouraged her to begin writing in high school, and she hasn't stopped since.

Determined to bring a new edge to romance, she continues to develop intriguing plots, racy characters and fresh dialogue—thus keeping readers on their toes! Visit her Web site at www.acarthur.net.

Second Chance, Baby

A.C. ARTHUR

KIMANI
ROMANCE

KIMANI PRESS™

ISBN-13: 978-0-373-86084-5
ISBN-10:   0-373-86084-6

Special thanks and acknowledgment to A.C. Arthur for her contribution
to The Braddocks: Secret Son miniseries.

SECOND CHANCE, BABY

Dear Reader,

Bringing Tyson and Felicia to life was a wonderful experience. I believe these two are the epitome of what makes a marriage work: love, prayer and compromise. The Braddocks are like any normal family struggling with the grief process, except they have the added pain of trying to figure out exactly what happened to their loved one.

A baby will be the second chance that Ty and Felicia need, but the legacy of Harmon Braddock will be the grounding force to keep them going.

I hope you enjoy this installment of the Braddocks!

A.C.

In Loving Memory of Minister Shelton L. Moore,
1952–2007
You will always have a very special place in my heart.

To Bernadette E. Moore
Love. Hope. Faith. May they all see you through.

Acknowledgments

A very special thanks to Adrianne Byrd for all the
brainstorming and chitchats about the Braddocks.

To Mavis Allen for recruiting me to be on this very special
project and to Kelli Martin for stepping in and making
this a great continuity.

Chapter 1

He couldn't get her out of his mind.

Tyson Braddock walked along the busy street without paying a bit of attention to his surroundings. He'd lived in Houston all his life, so he wasn't amazed by the sights. Besides, his mind was usually too preoccupied with business to take in the scenery. Today, however, it wasn't business that plagued him.

Anyone who knew Ty would be surprised by that fact alone.

At this moment there was just too much going on in his life. It was early October. The year was quickly coming to an end and Ty couldn't tell if he was glad or sad about it. It was natural to lean more toward sad since in the last nine months he'd had his wife walk out on him, his father die, his wife come back to him and then leave him again.

His dad's death... Ty was just beyond devastated.

Harmon Braddock had not only been an influential politician but a devoted husband and a family man. Except for the months leading up to his death, when his father had seemed preoccupied with something bigger than politics and his family combined. Ty hadn't paid that much attention, although he now admitted he should have.

Congressman Harmon Braddock had been a pillar of the community, a successful district attorney turned politician who had gained the adoration and respect of the majority of the town's citizens. The Braddock name was as close as you could get to royalty in Houston. So it was understandable that Harmon's accident and death would be newsworthy. Though Ty doubted the press knew of the inconsistencies.

Ty, Malcolm and Shondra had picked up on those inconsistencies and were now wondering what it all meant. Was their father killed? Was he involved in some type of political conspiracy? And if so, how were the three of them going to uncover the truth and seek justice for their father?

The Braddock children were determined to do just that.

Ty was the middle of three children. His older brother was Malcolm, the one his parents clearly expected to walk in Harmon's footsteps. His younger sister, Shondra, was beautiful and respected for her intelligence in her profession as a high-powered, successful management and compliance officer. Ty, true to middle-child syndrome, felt loved but burdened with the need to overachieve just to earn a distinct place in his family. He'd been born with money but felt compelled to make his mark in business on his own. So he'd spent his entire adult life focused on success in business. In that quest he was relentless.

Continuing his walk, Ty turned the corner, vaguely noticing people going in and out of the shops that lined the street. It was a crisp fall day and he deeply inhaled the fresh air. With his hands thrust in his pockets, Ty let himself remember one of the most painful nights of his life. The night he'd found out Harmon was dead.

Shondra, whom he and Malcolm still called by her childhood nickname, "Shawnie," had been the one to call him well after midnight. He had just gotten into bed after working on a proposal for Christopher Brentwood of Brentwood Holdings.

Shawnie hadn't given him much information except that their father's car had gone speeding out of control, flipping over and over before careening down an embankment. And that he needed to get to the hospital as soon as possible. By the time he'd arrived, his father was gone.

For days he'd functioned on sheer autopilot. His condo in the downtown area of Houston seemed even bigger and emptier. Almost like a tomb. And only six months before, his wife of five years had moved out.

Felicia taught first grade at the local elementary school. She loved it and so Ty tried not to press the issue about her staying home, no matter how much he wished she would. One evening he'd come home from work to find she was packed and gone. He'd talked to her a week later and she'd been adamant about the separation. Ty had been flabbergasted. They'd been so happy one day, then she was yelling and crying the next.

One thing he was absolutely certain of—he and Felicia were meant to be together. If she needed a few months to get over whatever it was she was going through, he was willing to give her that.

Except he hadn't anticipated his father's death or the strange feelings and yearnings that would come as a result.

Felicia Turner Braddock was compassionate and loyal. On the day of the funeral, when she had come walking back into his family home after six months of being away, he'd felt a soothing calm wash over him. Very little shock. It was like his body and soul had just been patiently waiting for her. She'd embraced him immediately, and Ty had known without a doubt that with her here he could make it through this day, and the next.

They'd returned to the penthouse after the last of the mourners had left the Braddock estate. The ride back into the city was quiet as Ty thought of the turn his life had taken in such a short span of time. He'd expected her to come back home with him and that they would get through this grief together.

So when they'd walked into the house and he'd gone directly into the bedroom, it was natural for her to follow him there. What had thrown him was the way she'd sat on the edge of the bed, her hands in her lap, as if this were her first time there.

Maybe she was having a moment. Ty had experienced plenty of them in the last week. He'd be doing something normal or mundane, and just like that his thoughts would drift to Harmon and the loss would seem too profound for words.

His fingers shook a little as he unbuttoned his shirt and stripped it off, tossing it to the floor. Then he'd had to sit down as the memories came fast, turning his insides once again to a jittery mess.

He'd felt her hand on his shoulder as she tried to comfort him. Then her arms were wrapped around him and he leaned into her embrace. It felt comfortable and different all at the same time.

She had trembled in his arms then sniffled. He'd brushed his hands through her hair, whispering something about them getting through this together.

Then the moment had shifted. Grief slipped aside, opening the door to a familiar rush of passion. His wife was in his arms, in his bed, a place she hadn't been in months, and he loved it.

Ty told himself that circumstances put them in this time and place, that he shouldn't take advantage. Yet his hands moved down her back to cup her bottom. It was instinctive. Her arms were wrapped around his back, her nails digging in slightly as he touched her.

In the next instant their mouths were joined, his lips moving over hers boldly, wickedly. She seemed to melt in his arms even as she stroked the intense heat building within him. Every touch, every moan, every movement felt right. It felt perfect.

They didn't speak. Words were no longer necessary. Each touch was a memory renewed. When he'd lifted the edge of her nightgown, pulling it up and over her head, he was entranced by her beauty that had only matured with her over the years. She was no longer the timid college girl he'd first taken to his bed. Now, she was an experienced lover, arching to his touch, moaning to his kiss. Anticipation bubbled just beneath the surface of his skin and he licked his lips impatiently.

It had always been this way between them, this hot rush of desire that didn't calm until he was deeply embedded inside her and they were both completely sated.

When she reached out, flattening her palms on his bare chest, Ty's entire body stiffened, then warmed. He wanted this woman with a desperation he'd never known before, needed her like nothing he'd ever needed in his life. Leaning forward, he kissed her with all the emotion swirling inside of him. He was gentle at first, because his one priority had been to always love and cherish her. Then his lips grew more persistent, his tongue slipping past her lips, her teeth, to claim her fully. Her tongue snaked along his and the dam broke free. Ty kissed her with pent-up urgency, conveying the fierceness of his love for her, his devotion and vow to protect and take care of her.

They'd loved each other in this way so many times before, it was second nature. When she lay naked on the bed, Ty could only look down at her, his mind reeling with emotion, his body edgy with need. She had only to lift her arms in invitation before he was slipping between her legs, entering her with one long thrust, one satisfied moan.

That moan was quickly replaced by tiny pants and heated growls as Ty created a rhythm and Felicia lifted her hips to match it. This was the connection he'd come to rely on, the one constant in his life—his love for this woman.

The next morning he'd gone to the office at his usual time, five o'clock. He'd called home a couple of hours later to see if Felicia had left for work and had received no answer. After several attempts on her cell, he figured he'd just see her later. But he was mistaken.

This time, at least, she'd left him a note. She wasn't going to stay with him. The night before had been wonderful but it had been a mistake. He couldn't give her what she wanted, so a separation was the best solution.

Ty had been livid. For the first time in years, he'd taken his frustration out on something besides the punching bag in his home gym. He'd burned the note then tossed a few choice pieces of artwork, watching them smash into the walls of the penthouse, enjoying the scene of them breaking. Just like his heart.

That had been three months ago. Ty hadn't seen nor heard from Felicia since then. He'd called her because he thought his marriage deserved that much. She'd refused his calls. He wasn't into begging, so the calls quickly stopped. For now. But in the weeks that passed he'd held on to the fact that he hadn't heard from any attorney on her behalf. That was a good sign. Because Ty had no intention of ever letting his wife go.

Felicia Turner Braddock's heart fluttered as she held the blanket up to her cheek. Burying her nose in it, she let its smell sift through the raging hormones in her body.

Her eyes misted and she blinked to keep from making a complete fool of herself inside this quaint shop. One of her co-workers had hipped her to the place and Felicia was ecstatic to find the woman was absolutely right. This shop was comfortable, fabulous and had everything she would need and then some.

Gently laying her hand on her lower stomach, Felicia sighed.

Ten years ago, when she'd first seen Tyson Braddock walking across the campus of Texas

A&M, she'd been enamored along with the rest of the female population at TAMU. Felicia prided herself on being one of the smartest of them all, though she knew a man as good-looking and inherently successful as Tyson would never be interested in a shy, quiet girl from South Texas. So she hadn't even bothered with the games and ploys the other girls performed to get his attention. By day she focused on school and getting her degree. And by night, in the privacy of her dorm room, she longed for him.

It was on a windy October night, days before Halloween. She'd been coming from a late study session in the library and Ty had bumped into her, knocking her and all her books to the ground. He'd been fooling around with some of his frat buddies and not watching where he was going. She'd been so tired from late-night studying and the part-time job she was working at the school bookstore that she wouldn't have seen a Mack truck if it had come barreling at her.

Embarrassed, angry and still tired as hell, she'd scrambled on the ground to pick up her books. Ty had been faster, collecting each textbook along with her notebook and her purse without a word. He'd offered her a hand up then because she was now on her knees wondering where the mess she'd dropped had gone. She looked up at him and could have sworn the sun was shining in a halo around him—except for the fact that it was close to midnight. Finally coming to her senses, she'd put her hand in his and let him help her up. As smart as she considered herself, she had no idea just how handsome he was close up.

He was tall and towered above her meager five feet four inches. She craned her neck to look up at him and was blinded by his smile. God, he was so fine it should have been a sin. He'd said something that snapped her out of her reverie and she remembered smiling and muttering a thank-you. She'd walked away so fast she would swear she was a blur in the wind.

The next morning he was waiting at the door of her dorm. And for the next two weeks he met her at each class and walked her home from her late-night studying at the library. Their meetings had been really casual. He talked of his family and everyday things while she, although still in awe, managed to talk about the same. A month later he asked her out on a real date. By this time Felicia had come to the conclusion that Tyson Braddock was not the all-American star athlete and untouchable sex symbol the girls on campus thought he was. Underneath the handsome and polished exterior, he was just a man who loved pizza and basketball, economics, vintage cars and R & B music. And he was kind, focused, and he truly seemed to care about her.

Ty and Felicia found they had a lot in common, and before either of them knew it they were an item, dating seriously and sending rumors flying around the campus. It wasn't the instant-fall-desperately-in-love like Nicky and Terry in one of Felicia's favorite movies *An Affair to Remember.* It was more like the intense, heated drop into sub-mission like Darius and Nina in *Love Jones,* an-other one of her all-time favorite chick flicks.

Marriage was obviously on their horizon and the fairy-tale ceremony their shining moment in the spotlight. She loved that man like nothing and no one in her life. And in the five years of their mar-riage, she'd given him everything she had physically and mentally. She'd also sacrificed the one thing she'd wanted most because he said he wasn't ready.

Until his excuses became the norm and she real-ized what he wasn't saying, but wholeheartedly meant, was that he didn't want children.

The hardest decision Felicia ever had to make was to walk away from her marriage, from the commitment she'd made before God and her par-ents. But she'd done so to save herself.

Ty came from a very influential family. He was rich even before he made his first million. His father, Harmon, was a congressman. His mother, Evelyn, was a philanthropist who worked specifically with hospitals and women's-rights organizations. His older brother, Malcolm, was the bleeding heart and had left the family, so to speak, a few years before to become a community activist. Malcolm was definitely the Braddock with a conscience and now he may follow in Harmon's political footsteps. While Shawnie was her father's daughter, with her brilliant mind and touch of rebellion, Tyson was the lone ranger of the family. The only one who did not hold a law degree, he was still the epitome of ambition. For that very reason, her marriage had never stood a chance.

In the beginning, their marriage was strong, but soon Tyson's career and his quest for success proved more important than she'd ever been. Felicia had finally grown tired of the competition.

Giving up was not usually in her nature, especially when it came to relationships. Her parents were very traditional and prided themselves on their long and enduring relationship. They would be heartbroken to learn that she hadn't had what it took to make hers work.

Still, she'd been strong the morning she packed

her bags and left the penthouse she and Ty had picked out and furnished together. She hadn't even left him a note that first time.

He was so smart, with his MBA degree and intuition, he should have been able to figure it out. Especially since the day before they'd argued about starting a family.

Her heart had ached until she'd thought about ripping it free to finally gain some peace. But later she'd received the news of Harmon's death. Felicia had grieved as if he were her own father. And despite the animosity she had toward Ty, she wouldn't have wished that tragedy on anyone. So it was with that in mind that she'd returned to the Braddock estate on the outskirts of Houston.

Being with the family again had been difficult, especially since she hadn't seen or spoken to any of them in more than six months. The moment she arrived, Ty made a point of telling her that he hadn't mentioned her hiatus to his family. Felicia had been stung by the way he'd called her departure a hiatus, like she'd gone on some type of vacation or something. But that hadn't been the time to get into it.

Besides, just seeing Ty again had her body and her emotions going haywire. A case in point was the passionate night they'd spent together after leaving the cemetery. Looking back now, Felicia had to claim that as one of the best nights of her life.

But then the next morning, it looked to Felicia as if it was business as usual for Ty, like he hadn't just buried his father. Like they hadn't made sweet, tender love to one another. When she'd tried to talk to him, he'd brushed her off. He was officially unreachable, emotionally closed off just as he'd been the last few years.

Now, walking around the store, Felicia sighed over all the different designs and the racks of clothes in a pastel rainbow of colors.

She heard the tiny bell that signaled a new customer entering the store, but didn't pay it much attention. But as she surveyed the outfits, her peripheral vision caught the suit and that confident swagger. Expensive and elegant, that's what it was, and when she raised her gaze a little higher, her heart pounded.

"Ty!" she gasped. As if she had been caught stealing, she thrust her arms with the clothes in hand behind her back.

"What are you doing here?" he asked, his medium brown eyes raking over her with barely masked hunger.

"I, um, I'm shopping." Lord, she prayed he wouldn't ask what or who she was shopping for.

"I've been calling you."

Felicia licked her lips nervously. "I know."

"Why haven't you returned my calls?"

"Ty, this is not the place to discuss this. I'll call you later."

His thick eyebrows drew close as he frowned. "I'm not inclined to believe that, since you've been ducking me for about three months now."

Felicia shifted uncomfortably beneath his gaze. Would she ever stop feeling like a love-struck college girl in his presence? She was grown and he'd hurt her, repeatedly, by ignoring her and denying what she wanted most in the world. By all normal standards, she should be able to walk away from him without a second thought. Yet, even now, she couldn't.

He took a step closer and touched a hand to her shoulder. "What's going on with you, Felicia? Why won't you just talk to me?"

She closed her eyes. His touch felt so good, but it was distracting her from the matter at hand. Taking a deep breath, she looked up at him. "I can't," she said, with all the strain and indecision she'd been feeling since leaving him the first time.

He rubbed her shoulder, an act she remembered all too well. "Yes, you can. We've always been able to talk. We're best friends. Remember you told me that the night of our graduation. There's nothing we can't say to each other."

That was then and this was now, Felicia thought dismally. Still, she was surprised he'd even remembered something like that. "Things have changed."

"Yeah, they have," he said, then, as if just noticing his surroundings, looked around the store and back at her. "What are you doing in a baby store?"

Even as the question left his lips, his hands moved around her back. He pulled her wrists around so that the clothes she was holding—two baby sleepers—were now hanging between them.

"What are these? A present for someone you know?"

His gaze lifted from the sleepers and met hers. For all she wanted to pick up and run out of that store, she knew the moment she'd been dreading had finally come.

"They're for a baby." She took a steadying breath. "Our baby."

Chapter 2

She did not just say "our baby," Ty's mind roared. "What the hell are you talking about?" he exclaimed.

Her upper body shook and Ty realized it was because he'd grasped her shoulders, shaking her with each word he'd spoken. Immediately disgusted with himself, he yanked his hands away from her. "I want to know what's going on right now, Felicia," he said through clenched teeth.

With movements too slow for his liking, Felicia turned, placing the baby clothes onto the rack behind her. When she turned back to him her warm brown eyes appeared glazed with tears. "Let's not do this here," she said quietly.

Ty had to take a deep breath. His emotions were swirling through his body, pain and confusion burning through the layers of other stress he was currently dealing with. He recognized that this was not the place to air their dirty laundry. People would undoubtedly recognize him and the last thing his family needed right now was some trifling gossip about him and his estranged wife in a baby store.

"Fine. Let's go." He reached for her hand and wasn't surprised that she didn't readily give it to him. With a long sigh, he took her hand, albeit gently, and led her out of the store.

Across the street was a bistro. It looked like one of those French shops with the awning trimmed in some curling material. Houston's typical cold front, which signaled the official shift from autumn to winter, hadn't yet hit, so small tables with fancy-backed white chairs were still set outside for customers. He bypassed the host with a nod then proceeded directly to a table in the shade. Pulling out her chair, he watched as Felicia sat down. Her scent, that perfume she loved so much from Clinique, wafted up through his nostrils. God, he missed her.

Taking a seat across from her, Ty tried valiantly not to yell again. She'd just said *our baby,* meaning theirs—his and hers. When had she gotten pregnant? And when had she planned to tell him?

Before speaking, he looked at her closely. She looked tired but even that didn't hamper her beauty, or the added glow he noted around her cheeks. Her honey-brown complexion was accented by high cheekbones and wide, expressive eyes. How many nights had he stared into those eyes and pledged his undying love?

His gaze fell to her breasts and his mouth watered. He'd always loved her body. She was small, but curvy and soft in all the right places.

Ty had dubbed her his sweetheart and vowed to always protect her from any harm or danger. But the way she was looking at him made Ty feel as if the person she needed protection from was him. Traveling farther down, he saw that the top she wore, which fitted across her bodice, flared from a band of material at her rib cage. There was no real sign of a pregnant stomach but the blouse was a lot looser than Felicia's normal attire.

She was pregnant. That realization hit him with warm finality. Having children had been a few years off in his life plan. Yet, Harmon's immortality had him lately thinking of family. A lot.

"It was the night of the funeral," she said when he continued to watch her.

Lifting his gaze to her face, he marveled at the soft auburn curls of her hair that rested so adoringly at her shoulders. Her round, cherublike face, full lips and soulful eyes bore into him. "Why did you leave?" he asked with his emotions clogging his throat.

She sighed and sat back in the chair. "We're not on the same page anymore, Ty. You know that. You want your business and I want…more."

"I want you," he said without hesitation.

She tilted her head to the side. "We can't always have what we want."

He clenched his teeth. For as sweet as Felicia was, she could be just as stubborn as he. "You had no right to keep a secret like this." If there was one thing Ty hated, it was secrets. They had a way of coming back to haunt you. Or slap you in the face. "Did you ever plan to tell me about my child?"

Felicia looked offended. "Of course I was going to tell you. I would never keep you away from your child. Even if you don't want one. I just didn't want you to think I was trying to trap you or something."

He shook his head in disbelief. "First off, I never said I didn't want a child."

"You never said you did. And besides that,

actions speak louder than words, Ty. Working twenty hours a day, weekends included, barely having time to eat dinner with me, let alone make love to me, said it all."

"It wasn't like that. It was just never the right time."

"Oh, really? Then tell me what it was like. For you, I mean. Did you really think we had a good marriage?" Her hands had been waving as she spoke, a sure sign that this conversation was about to get very emotional.

"Sure there were rough days, but that was normal. I thought we were both getting what we wanted."

She folded her arms over her chest. "No. You were getting what you wanted. I was just taking up space."

Ty let her words marinate and tried like hell to hold on to his temper. How could she sit here and use his actions to justify why she hadn't told him about his child?

On another note, there could be some truth to her words. He did work a lot, but that was for the good of them both, for their future. He wanted them to be financially secure, outside of the Braddock fortune. Working hard was the only way a man could adequately provide for his family. He'd learned that from his father.

All this past mumbo jumbo aside, Ty was not

about to let Felicia raise his baby without him. "I want you back, Felicia. I never wanted you to leave."

"Ty." She sighed.

The shreds of his calm shattered and he slammed his hands down on the table. "You will not shut me out of this pregnancy or my child's life, no matter what you think you know about me!"

"Keep your voice down," she said sternly, as if he were one of her students.

Ty dragged a hand down his face. His temples hurt like hell. "I don't know what you want me to say, what you want me to do, Felicia."

"Like I said, what I wanted never mattered to you." When he was about to say something else, she held up a hand to stop him. "Now that you know, I will keep you in the loop about the pregnancy. You can be a father to your child."

"Thanks for the permission," he snapped.

She frowned. "Don't do that."

"Don't do what? Don't act pissed off? Well, I am. So deal with it." How dare she keep this from him? And how dare she act like she was doing him a favor by *allowing* him to be in his child's life? They were once so happy. How had they come to this?

"That's just it, Ty. I *have* been dealing with it. I've been dealing with you and your twisted priorities and your lack of attention. But I don't have to take it."

Her words were curt, sharp and sounded entirely too final for his liking. "So what are you saying? You don't want to be with me?" Asking the question made him feel vulnerable and insufficient. Sitting up straighter, he cleared his throat. "We took vows, Felicia. And I for one didn't take them lightly. There are problems in every marriage. The true test is loyalty and patience. Does our love mean so little to you that you won't even try?"

No, the hell he wasn't! she thought.

He was *not* turning the tables on her, making this all seem like her fault. She'd tried and tried. Talking and planning romantic weekends and trying to bring back the spark they'd once had. All to no avail.

"You were the one who stopped trying, Ty. Your job always came first. Making your next million meant more than making love to your wife. And you expected me to simply be there to help you celebrate. I won't be your trophy wife. It takes two to make a marriage work."

He touched his fingers to his temples and rubbed. He had a headache and Felicia immediately felt guilty. Ty always got headaches when he was hungry or tired. She could guess what the culprit was this time. Opening her purse, she dug inside and pulled out a bottle of ibuprofen. "You haven't eaten today, have you?"

"What?" he asked, his eyes squinting as he looked at her.

"Food? Did you have any? Breakfast, lunch? Never mind." She opened the bottle and poured two pills into her hand. Signaling the waiter, she ordered them two glasses of water and salads. The water came first and she put the pills in Ty's hand.

He didn't say a word but popped the pills and lifted the glass to drink.

"Three meals a day can easily be woven into your work schedule. How do you expect to keep up your strength if you forget to eat? You are not Superman," she said, watching him swallow.

He chuckled. "I was your Superman once."

Felicia had to smile at that one, touched once again by the sentiment in his tone. She hadn't heard him talk like that in years. "Yes, you were. A long time ago."

When he reached across the table for her hand, she didn't pull away. "I want what we had before, Felicia. I want you with me again. If that means I have to change some things, then I will. But this separation is killing me. It's been three whole months!"

Run? Stay? Her mind argued even as his thumb rubbed over the back of her hand. Heat moved swiftly up her arm and settled throughout her chest with familiarity.

She sighed. "It's not that easy. You can't just say you want it and think that it will be. I wanted it all for us, Ty. The careers, the family, the love."

"I've never stopped loving you."

"You just stopped being with me."

"How can I fix this?" he implored with a look of such honesty that it almost broke her heart.

"I only wanted you and a life where we were equal partners and friends. I wanted a family and a home."

He nodded as if hearing her for the first time. "I understand."

"Do you really?" she asked.

"I know exactly what you need, Felicia. I always have," he said with that slow, sinful smile.

Felicia's insides melted. Boy, did he know what she needed. Flashes of their last night together hit her like a warm breeze.

When it came to the bedroom—or any room, for that matter—Ty knew and always delivered everything she wanted or needed. But that area of their lives wasn't the problem. When he wasn't working, his performance in bed was much more than she could ask for. However, their marriage could not survive on sex alone. She shook her head to clear her thoughts, then put her hand on her belly and thought about her own family.

She was an only child. Her parents, Marshall and Lydia Turner, had been happily married for forty-three years. They had a loving, trusting marriage—one that was filled with arguments and makeups, trials and tribulations, but one they both cherished. They'd been her role models as she'd grown up. She wanted a marriage just like theirs. And she wasn't settling for anything less.

"That's not what I'm talking about, Ty. Sex was never a problem for us."

"No. And apparently we've had much more success than I'd anticipated," he said, nodding toward her belly. "I can't believe we're going to have a baby."

She smiled, hoping he really was excited, but she wasn't really sure. She knew a baby wasn't a part of Ty's plan just yet. But there wasn't much they could do about it now. "When the doctor told me, I was in a state of shock for days."

They both grew quiet. "I was so sorry about Harmon's death, and then this happened, and I just didn't know how to tell you. I didn't know how you would react."

"You can tell me anything, baby. Don't ever forget that."

Felicia looked at this man and knew that she loved him even more today than she ever had. He'd been her best friend for almost ten years and her lover for more than half that time. Of course she could tell him anything, but could she trust him again with her heart?

"Let's have dinner tonight? At the penthouse."

"I'm not moving back in, Ty. If you really want a reconciliation, you're going to have to prove it. You're going to have to convince me that we should give this another try."

He stared at her a moment, contemplating— she could tell by the slight furrow of his brow.

"So you won't move back in until I prove to you that we can make this work?" He nodded, answering himself. "I can do that. I can win you back, if that's what you want."

Leave it to Ty to make everything a competition. Ambition infected his blood like a disease. "I'm just saying that I've spent a lot of time trying to rekindle the spark between us, trying to bring back what we lost somewhere along the road. I'm not willing to do it this time. You're going to have to do the trying."

"Fine. Dinner tonight at the penthouse."

He grinned devilishly and she groaned. "No sex, Ty."

Ty cleared his throat. "No sex. I just want to share a meal with you, like we used to."

She sighed. Looking into his eyes, having him touch her…she never stood a chance.

Felicia stood at the door to the home she and Ty had shared, debating whether or not she should use her key. Still, she needed to retain some sort of distance between them. As she'd told Ty earlier that afternoon, she wasn't about to run back to him and things the way they were, baby or not. She wasn't about to act like things were even remotely back to normal.

After a few more awkward moments, she realized how foolish she was being and lifted her hand to ring the doorbell. Ty was at the door in no time, as if he'd been standing directly on the other side waiting for her.

"Hey, you're right on time, as always." He smiled and Felicia almost bolted.

How was she going to survive having dinner with him, here of all places? It was bad enough she'd been thinking of him and that crazy toned body for the duration of the afternoon. "I was hungry." She shrugged and walked inside.

"I'll bet, considering your present condition. Let me get that for you." He took her purse and the sweater she'd draped over her arm as a weather precaution.

Felicia continued into the living area. She loved their loft-style penthouse and remembered each piece of furniture they'd chosen together. Clean lines and a contemporary décor was their goal. As she stood in front of the wall-length windows, she would say they'd hit their mark.

Ty wanted to be close to the pulse of the business industry, and so they'd found this great place in the center of downtown. The windows that made up one wall overlooked downtown Houston's Near Northside.

As dusk had just settled over the city, Felicia was treated to the sultry golden hue of the sun as it settled for the night. Buildings glowed majestically, while trees with leaves just changing color filled the landscape. In the distance the Quitman Bridge had a steady flow of commuters either heading toward Houston's nightlife or hurrying to get home and put the workday behind them. Folding her arms, she took a moment to simply enjoy.

"You look good standing there," Ty said from behind.

She turned slowly. "It's the view."

He shook his head. "No. It's you. I always liked to see you standing there looking so content."

Quickly unfolding her arms, she moved away

from the window to take a seat on the beige leather couch. "Looks can be deceiving."

Ty didn't respond, but came to sit beside her. "Dinner's just about done. Do you want to listen to some music?"

Felicia blinked in surprise as he leaned forward and picked up the remote to the entertainment center from the cherrywood block coffee table. When was the last time she and Ty had simply sat in the living room listening to music? When was the last time they had sat and did anything together?

She watched in a trance as he pushed buttons, having never mastered that monstrosity he called a remote. It operated everything electronic in the room—the DVD, the CD player, the television, etc. It had been her practice to just push the power button on the machine she wanted to turn on. The remote was intimidating and entirely Ty's domain.

Her heart stumbled when the first chords of a song she hadn't heard for years began to play. It was an old Freddie Jackson song she and Ty had listened to as they'd studied back in college. She couldn't help but smile. "Where'd you find that?"

It was Ty's turn to shrug. "It wasn't lost, just forgotten for a while."

She sat back in the chair, loving the caramel and

ivory pillows she'd insisted on. The relaxing was good for her. Dr. Franz, her ob-gyn, had informed her that during her first trimester she should try and get as much rest as possible. Especially in light of the mild cramping she experienced erratically. Dr. Franz said it wasn't a big deal as long as she wasn't bleeding or the pain didn't become unbearable. But she certainly wanted to be as careful as she could.

"Are you comfortable?" Ty asked. "Can I get you something to drink?"

"Please, no." She chuckled, shaking her head. "I go to the bathroom enough without any added help."

"Really? I always thought that was later in the pregnancy."

"Nope. That was one of those symptoms that started right away. I hear it gets worse as the baby grows. I'm definitely not looking forward to more trips to the bathroom."

"So you've been to the doctor and everything is going to be okay? You and the baby are healthy?"

She couldn't help but touch her stomach at his words. In the beginning of their marriage, Ty had always been very attentive, providing any- and everything she needed—from a glass of wine when they came home from work to a massage on those particularly rough days she'd had at school.

"Dr. Franz said that everything looks fine. He anticipates a noneventful pregnancy and a healthy baby in late April."

To her surprise, Ty smiled. "May I?" he asked, nodding at the spot on her stomach where her hand rested.

After a second of stunned silence, she smiled. "Sure. There's not much to feel yet."

When his hand replaced hers, Felicia's pulse quickened. It wasn't just with the awareness that it had been almost three months since she'd felt Ty's hands on her. It was also the realization that what he was feeling was something they'd both created. The baby that would forever symbolize their love and commitment. Family.

"This still seems a little unreal," he said, his eyes glued to her stomach.

"Is that good or bad?" she inquired tentatively.

He lifted his gaze to hers and smiled with complete sincerity. "It's perfect."

Keeping his palm on her stomach, Ty continued to stare at her. He used to do that when they were in college. She'd be reading some textbook and assuming he was doing the same. But when she'd look up, those intense, dark brown eyes would be focused solely on her. What was it he used to say he was doing?

"I'm still memorizing you," he said as if he'd read her mind. "After all these years, I look at you and want the picture of your face to stay permanently etched in my mind."

Dammit. She wasn't going to make it. He was pushing all the right buttons, saying all the right things. How could she resist coming back to him?

"I wonder why that is, Ty. I mean, I've always wondered why you'd want to memorize me. Is it that you knew one day we would part?" Clearly Ty hadn't expected that, as his once-soft gaze shifted to mildly irritated.

"I don't want tonight to go this way, Felicia. I want us to spend the evening together, with nothing on our minds but you and me. Like we used to do."

She nodded, chastising herself for being a little insensitive. It was a protective instinct, she knew, but was it necessary?

"I hear you."

"Let's just relax and not think about our issues for this one night."

He moved closer as he spoke, his voice lowering to that seductive tone she knew all too well. Still, she heard what he was saying and decided it wasn't such a bad idea.

"That sounds perfect," she whispered, just before his lips brushed hers.

* * *

Tonight is going to go well, Ty thought with certainty. He had the music and her favorite meal: meat loaf, mashed potatoes and corn. Ty was used to getting his way, and in this arena there would be no changing that. He would win his wife back, and then he'd make sure she never felt she had to leave him again.

After dropping Felicia off at the school this afternoon, he'd thought of her constantly. However, when he'd arrived back at his office, Shondra had called to see if he was available for lunch with her and Malcolm tomorrow, and he'd been forced to think of his father's death again.

He knew the story of how long his parents had tried for children; it had been years before his mother had gotten pregnant. They had just been about to give up. The appearance of him, his brother and his sister brought a sense of completion to their lives. He realized that with Felicia now carrying his child, he wanted that same thing. His dad was gone, and now Ty wanted to leave his own legacy.

He wanted his career, his wife, his child, his family. And nothing was going to stop him from having them. He hadn't been so sure of anything in a long, long while.

* * *

"Dinner was fantastic," Felicia said when they stood out on the balcony. "How much did you pay Sarona to cook it for you?" Because Felicia knew nothing if she didn't know her man. Sarona, the Braddocks' longtime housekeeper, cooked like an angel. Felicia would know her signature mashed potatoes anywhere.

"I'm offended." He smiled and leaned against the railing. "You know I can cook."

"Shrimp pizza and hamburgers on the grill are the extent of your culinary expertise. This was a good soul food meal that you definitely did not prepare yourself."

"All right. All right, you caught me. But I had the best intentions."

"You did, so you earn points for effort," she said, watching as the crisp, white dress shirt, left unbuttoned at the neck, molded his upper body.

Ty had always been sexy. There was no doubt about that. Even in the designer suits he seemed to wear more than anything else, he exuded pure, unadulterated sex appeal. She'd been thinking of nothing else but heading to the bedroom with her gorgeous husband for the duration of the night. Her hormones were going crazy. Luckily her brain still had some power over her libido.

While she'd been lusting after his body, Ty had moved closer so that his hand was now caressing her cheek. His cologne permeated her senses. She looked away, pretending that the view from the balcony was affecting her more than the man standing too damn close to her.

Putting a fingertip to her chin, he directed her gaze back to him. "You can't walk away from me, from us," he whispered, his face looming dangerously close to hers.

"Ty," she whispered, trying to turn away from him. She knew what was coming, and no matter how much she wanted it, she knew that it would be a mistake. That kiss they'd shared before dinner had been brief but still potent enough to leave her off-kilter.

"I love you so much, Felicia."

At his words, she could do nothing more than sigh. "You said we would take this slow."

"We're not supposed to do this tonight. Just dinner, remember?"

He feigned innocence, which was a blatant lie considering that devilish look in his eyes. "We're not doing anything." His lips touched hers in a sweeping fashion that sent tingles all the way to her toes.

Her body was instantly on fire, her tongue anticipating the silky feel of his. "This doesn't solve our problems."

"No," he answered, then used his tongue to stroke fire into her mouth, pulling out the moment she was about to give in. "But it's a damn good start to our reconciliation."

He wasn't lying about that, Felicia thought with a groan. Then she felt her body leaning into his. His arms wrapped quickly around her, locking her in place. "You're not playing fair," she gasped, then nipped his bottom lip, loving the scrape of his low-trimmed goatee against her face.

"All's fair in love and war." He sighed a second before taking her mouth in a scorching kiss that made her remember just why she'd spent the last nine years loving this man.

Chapter 3

Shawnie had gotten involved with Stewart Industries as a result of the siblings' amateur investigation into the death of their father. Malcolm and his
fiancée, Gloria Kingsley—who used to be his
father's assistant—had uncovered the fact that
Harmon's last cell phone call was made to someone
named Daiyu Longwei, who worked in the human
resources department at Stewart Industries.

Shawnie wasn't supposed to fall in love with the
owner of the major oil company, but looking at the
two of them across the table, Shondra's darker
complexion against Connor's lighter one, proved

Ty wrong. His sister was definitely in love. And, truth be told, Ty didn't begrudge her one moment of happiness. He and Felicia had been like that once, and after the previous night, Ty was sure they were on their way to that point again.

"Connor, did you find out anything about this Longwei person?" Ty asked. He had to get his mind off how happy his sister and Connor looked and fight the urge to call his wife.

Connor was able to look away from Shawnie for a moment to answer the question. "She's worked at the company for thirty-two years, after a foreign exchange internship while she was in college. In that time, she's moved up from an HR assistant to vice president of the entire department. Her employment file is squeaky clean. I haven't approached her personally yet. If she was the last person that Harmon called, she may have something to hide and is probably not real keen on being questioned. I don't want her to run before we get the information we need. So I'm trying to find an official reason to call her into my office for a conversation."

Shawnie shifted and crossed her long legs, to Connor's obvious delight. "I wonder if she was the same person who called Gloria? Remember? The one where the caller said it wasn't an accident."

Malcolm took a sip of his lemonade and shrugged.

"Gloria checked the caller ID but it read unavailable."

"Was she able to find out anything about Ms. Longwei from Dad's records?" Shawnie asked.

"No. There was nothing in his files about her. Not even an old message. Gloria has never heard the woman's name before, and you know how close she worked with Dad. If anybody would know Dad's connection to this woman it would be Gloria."

"That's true. Why didn't Gloria join us for lunch today?" Ty asked.

"She's down at the police station. The cops wanted a list of anything that might be missing from Dad's office after the break-in," Malcolm answered.

"Really? She found something missing?" Ty asked.

Malcolm shook his head. "No. But she wanted to go and tell them in person in case they had some other leads to tell her about."

"And you let her go by herself?" Shawnie inquired.

Connor answered before Malcolm had a chance. "That was probably smarter. A Braddock at the police station might set the reporters off."

Ty looked from Connor to Malcolm, who was nodding his agreement, and back to Connor again. Was it just a few short weeks ago that he and

Malcolm had walked in on the ridiculously rich white man kissing their baby sister? And now look at them, he thought, all sitting at a table having lunch and discussing his father's case. But Ty knew Connor was a cool guy, especially after he had discovered they both shared a love of cars. Connor's tastes, though, leaned more toward the expensive, speedy sports cars, compared to Ty's passion with vintage excellence.

"That's true. I'm glad we're all in agreement that this investigation is still on the down-low," Ty said.

Connor nodded. "Like I said before, I want to help you get to the bottom of this. Something is definitely not right. The phone call warning to Gloria, the response she got to stay away, the break-in and her last-minute travel plans to D.C. the day he died… The things you've uncovered so far support that notion. Besides, it's not that far-fetched that there's been a cover-up. That's the name of the game in politics these days."

"You've got that right," Malcolm chimed in. "That's why we need to be extra careful in the investigation."

"Let's face it, guys, we don't have a clue what we're doing here," Shondra said as she forked her salad. "I mean, we're grasping at straws, accumulating information but have no idea what to do with it."

"So what do you suggest?"

Shondra picked up her glass, drank and used a napkin to wipe her mouth. "Well, Mom did tell us to hire a PI, and Drey St. John offered to help."

The men exchanged weary glances.

"What do you know about him?" Malcolm asked Ty.

Ty shrugged. "Nothing much. He was at the funeral. He introduced himself, said he knew Dad and worked with him frequently. That's about it."

"Gloria said she has invoices that prove Dad employed him often. He's a private investigator. What more could we ask?"

Malcolm looked alarmed. "When did you talk to Gloria?"

Shondra was lifting another forkful of salad to her mouth. Ty had often wondered how the girl stayed so thin. Ever since she hit puberty she'd been able to eat just as much as he and Malcolm and still possessed a model's figure.

"She called me this morning. Why?"

"I don't like you two teaming up, that's why," Malcolm chided.

"Oh, please," Shondra quipped. "You're just afraid she might let it slip how you act in bed."

Ty and Connor laughed while Malcolm tried to suppress a grin. The older brother normally had a dry sense of humor, but Ty had noticed a change in Malcolm since Harmon's death. The change since he'd admitted his feelings for Gloria. Malcolm was light and unburdened these days. Ty was happy for his big brother, happy for the new direction Malcolm's life was taking.

"I'll try and talk to Ms. Longwei before the week is out. I'll call you guys with what I find out and you can decide what to do from there," Connor said.

Ty had emptied his own glass and signaled for the waitress to bring him lemonade. "That sounds good, Connor. Why don't we hold off on hiring St. John until we see if this Longwei has some relevant information?"

"She obviously knows that Dad's death wasn't an accident," Shondra said with a frown.

"Not necessarily," Malcolm interjected. "She could simply be making assumptions."

"Or," Ty added, "she may be involved in whatever is going on. In that regard, Connor, you need to be really careful about questioning her. We don't know what can of worms we're about to open up."

"You're right," Connor agreed.

Shondra and Malcolm agreed, as well.

"In the meantime, there's a cop at the gym where I work out. I can make some casual comments about the accident just to see if they're still looking into it. The guy and I are pretty cool, so he might just let something slip."

"You be careful, too," Shondra said. "You know corruption rarely skips the police department."

Ty nodded. "True."

They continued eating and talking, covering a range of subjects, one of which was their mother, Evelyn. They were all concerned about how she was taking Harmon's death, so Malcolm and Ty agreed to go and check up on her once Shondra and Connor left.

"Ty, tell Felicia I'll call her so we can get back into our lunch ritual," Shawnie said as they walked away. Ty and Malcolm rode in Malcolm's Mercury Mariner Hybrid through the city streets and got onto the highway that would lead them to the outskirts of the city, where the Braddock estate was. Ty liked his brother's truck but wasn't impressed by its size or new-age technology. He favored the old, tried-and-true vehicles and was looking forward to taking one of his favorites—the vintage teal 1963 Chevrolet Corvette he kept in the garage at the estate—out for a spin. It had been a while since he'd indulged in his only other hobby besides work. In truth, it had been too long.

Ty enjoyed the scenery as Malcolm drove. He

thought about his wife and their evening together. They must have kissed on that balcony for hours. All he knew for certain was that when he'd finally had to walk her to the door, his body was hard as steel and he was needing her more than he'd ever had in his life.

But Felicia had held to her word. She didn't want them to rush things. She wanted the whole dating, courting, whatever-you-wanted-to-call-it routine all over again. Ty wasn't really down for the waiting to sleep with her again—especially since they were already legally married and he'd gotten her pregnant—but he knew enough to give her what she wanted in that regard. He was looking at his marriage like a business deal now: it needed to be handled delicately until the final contracts were signed—the "final contracts" being the moment Felicia moved back in with him. That thought made him smile.

"What are you over there smiling about?" Malcolm asked. "You must have made another million or something, you look so happy."

Ty cleared his throat and pretended to adjust his seat belt. "Nah, it's nothing. Just enjoying the scenery."

"Man, you can't see anything but asphalt and cars driving too fast to get to someplace that's probably not all that important. That is not what put that smile on your face. So what's up?"

"It's nothing really. Just that things have been bad for a few months and they're finally starting to look a little better."

"You mean you and Felicia?"

"Why would you say that?" Ty asked. He'd been careful not to let anyone in his family know about his and Felicia's separation. For all they knew, she was just spending more time working and with her family. Her appearance at the funeral had helped tremendously, as both his mother and Shondra were happy to see her.

"Come on, Ty. I know you, and I know when something's bothering you. You were on edge even before Dad's death. I assumed it was about your wife since your business is doing so well. Felicia is the only thing you love more than work and your cars."

Ty thought about his brother's words for a moment, searching for and accepting the truth in them. "Things were a little shaky with us for a while. But now we're cool."

"Shaky, how?" Malcolm persisted.

Ty sighed, knowing his brother could be just as stubborn as him. That was one trait they'd all inherited from Harmon. They weren't going to make the additional twenty minutes of this ride without him telling Malcolm all he wanted to know, so there was no need in even trying.

"She left me," Ty said quietly.

"What? She left? Why?"

"I don't really know. I mean, I think I know now. But when it happened, I had no idea."

Malcolm shook his head. "That doesn't sound right."

"She left right after the New Year. I came home one day and she was gone. Then the day of the funeral she showed up. I thought things were back to normal, that whatever she'd been going through was fixed. So we slept together."

"But?"

"I didn't say *but.*"

Malcolm chuckled. "Still, I know there's one coming."

"*But* apparently things still weren't okay. She left again. I tried to call her. I left messages at her job and on her cell. I didn't even know where she was staying."

"Did you call her parents?"

"No."

"Why?"

"The same reason I didn't tell any of you. I didn't want them to know. Marriage is sacred to Felicia. Marshall and Lydia have been together for a long time and they have a great relationship. I didn't think she would run to them and tell them she was giving up on ours."

"So what's going on now?"

Ty thought for a moment. He rarely went for walks, especially during a weekday when he should have been working. But had he not been coming down that street, had he not glanced inside that store, he wouldn't be feeling as content as he was now. "I saw her yesterday."

Malcolm glanced at Ty, then back at the road. "You did? Where? Did you go to her job like some stalker?"

Ty frowned, offended that his brother would even suggest such a thing. "I wouldn't do that."

"I know you wouldn't. That's why you haven't spoken to or seen your wife in months." Malcolm chuckled. "You're too cool to show your emotions that way."

"What's that supposed to mean?"

"Just tell me what happened when you saw her."

Ty decided he wanted this conversation over with sooner rather than later, so he dismissed Malcolm's comment. "She's pregnant."

"What! It's yours, right?"

"Don't play games, Malcolm. Of course it's mine. She *is* my wife." And if Ty knew one thing about Felicia, it was that she was loyal. She would never step out on him, no matter how bad things were. As long as they were legally married—and this was true for him, as well—there would be no sleeping with anybody else.

"I can't tell," Malcolm said flippantly.

"All right, what's that supposed to mean? And I want a straight answer."

Malcolm shrugged. "I don't have a problem giving you one, little brother. You've been working and working since the day you and Felicia got married. You know why she left? Because she didn't think you'd miss her one way or another."

Ty opened his mouth to speak then quickly closed it again.

"Yeah, you know I'm right. Felicia's the type of woman that needs attention, Ty, and you weren't giving it to her. You better be thanking the good Lord that she's carrying your baby and not some other man's."

"Just because you're driving doesn't mean I won't hit you. Watch what you say about my wife."

Malcolm chuckled. "Don't get mad at me. I'm just keeping it real. There's more to life than work. It took me a while to realize that, but I see it clearly now. Felicia wants more than just money in the bank, Ty. She wants the whole fairy tale."

"I know what my wife wants, thank you very much." Ty shifted in his seat. "This all sounds real professional coming from a man who's been running from a serious commitment most of his adult life."

"I'm not downplaying my faults. But I'm wiser now."

"You mean you're Gloria-whipped now."

"Whatever." Malcolm laughed. "But seriously, I think you really need to think about what I've said and listen to what I'm sure Felicia's saying. She's pregnant now, man. It's time for you to take your marriage and your family more seriously than your job."

"If I don't work, how do I support my family?"

"Ty, you're not destitute. You have more money than most men twice your age. Besides, it's not all about the money. It's about living your life before it's too late. Don't you want to be there for Felicia and for your child?"

"Of course I do. And I will. That's why I have to work—to make sure they have everything they need all the time."

"I'm betting that all they're going to need is you," Malcolm said seriously.

"Thanks for the advice, big brother, but I've got this under control."

Malcolm shrugged and Ty hoped he was going to let it rest for now. "I don't have to tell you that this conversation goes no further than you and me."

"I'm not an idiot, Ty. Mom doesn't need this type of drama right now, and Shawnie's so in love with Connor that she couldn't care less what the rest of us are doing."

Ty smiled. "Yeah, that's weird as hell to see, isn't it?"

"It's borderline nasty. I'm going to have to keep my distance."

"Don't hate—you and Gloria are like that, too. I've seen you."

It was Malcolm's turn to smile. "Whatever."

Felicia had one hour to do class planning every day. While her first-graders were in gym, she sat behind her desk and reread the afternoon's reading lesson. She was just beginning the slippery trek into phonics and needed to remain focused. Twenty six-year-olds were full of energy and inquisitiveness. Neither of which made them ready to focus on learning to read.

She rearranged the flash cards with the sight words she would start with, and a memory from the past sneaked up on her.

She and Ty were back in school. He'd been studying for an exam in his literature class. Ty was a whiz with numbers but hated reading classic literature or poetry. So she'd come up with the idea to write the poet's name on one side of the card and a passage from one of his/her more notable works on the other.

They were in her dorm, she lying across her bed while Ty sat on the floor dribbling a basketball with the finesse of an NBA player. She'd flash him a card. His dark eyes would shift away from his hand and the ball for just a second, and then he'd recite the passage on the other side of the card. It had been when she'd flashed the card that read "Lady Montagu" and his immediate, unwavering response had been, "The man who feels the dear disease, Forgets himself, neglects to please, The crowd avoids, and seeks the groves, And much he thinks when much he loves." At that very moment Felicia knew without a doubt she was in love with him.

He'd spoken the words with such sincerity, such heartfelt honesty, that she'd believed he was speaking them directly to her instead of simply reciting the passage from memory.

"Can I put the names on the board for rec time, Mrs. Braddock?"

The high-pitched voice of one of her students

interrupted the memory, and Felicia cleared her throat.

"Madeline, what are you doing here? You're supposed to be in gym." Madeline Yi was a precocious, cheerful girl of Asian descent. Her inky hair, adorable round cheeks and inquisitive nature were a highlight to Felicia's day.

"I got my good shoes on so I can't pissisipate," Madeline said, her tongue slipping through the gap where her two front teeth used to be.

Felicia looked down to see that the child did, in fact, have on a lovely pair of patent leather shoes. Totally unsuitable for playing dodgeball. "The word is *participate,*" she gently corrected while standing up behind her desk. "We'll have to find something for you to do then."

"I can put the names on the board for rec," Madeline insisted.

"No. I'll do that."

"Why?"

"Because I'm the teacher," Felicia answered as the little girl followed her around the classroom.

"But I can be your helper."

"Yes. You can. And I'm going to find something for you to help me with." Felicia continued to look around her cheerfully decorated classroom for an assignment. She could have Madeline reorder the numbers for their leapfrog calendar, or she could put Madeline in charge of the booklets for the phonics lesson. However, she got the impression that Madeline was sure of what she wanted to do.

"But I want to help you put the names on the board for rec."

Felicia turned, too quickly, because Madeline bumped into her the moment she did. "Excuse me," she said, staring down into the child's serious expression.

Madeline nodded, her bone-straight hair gently brushing her shoulders.

"What's so special about the names on the rec board, Madeline?" Felicia asked.

The child remained quiet. A sure sign that something was going on. Stooping down until she was eye level with the child, Felicia said in her best, no-nonsense-but-compassionate voice, "Tell me the truth. Why do you want to put the names on the board?"

Madeline's thin lips protruded but Felicia did not waver. She continued to stare at her student expectantly. Until poor Madeline couldn't hold it a moment longer.

"That dirty Jimmy Petri called me a name in gym class, so he doesn't get any rec time." Madeline had said this on one long breath then folded her arms over her chest, clearly indignant about the whole affair.

Felicia tried to hide her smile. Jimmy Petri was a little boy with the biggest green eyes she'd ever seen and a head topped with golden curls. All the kids called him dirty because he had a tendency to pick his nose and not wash his hands. Felicia had unsuccessfully been working with Jimmy on this unsanitary habit of his but recognized it was age-appropriate behavior. One day, Felicia was sure, the same girls that unmercifully teased Jimmy were going to be head over heels in love with him, because his boyish cuteness was definitely going to flourish into one handsome man.

"Now, Madeline, Jimmy's mother didn't name him 'dirty,' so I need for you to stop calling him that. It isn't polite."

The child look appalled. "It's not polike for him to pick his nose, Mrs. Braddock."

Again Felicia held a chuckle, a hand involuntarily going to her stomach. It was moments like these that made her long to be a mother. She couldn't wait to have her own child. Ty's child.

"No, it's not, Madeline. But I'm sure Jimmy will stop that soon. Now, what name did he call you?"

Madeline tapped one patent leather shoe

while giving Felicia a look of pure impatience. "He called me a pampered princess so I hate him!" she said with a statement-making stomp of her foot.

Madeline's parents were wealthy and did spoil her rotten. But who could blame them? Felicia thought. The little girl was adorable. Still, a parent's spoiling could lead to potentially obnoxious children in the long run. Felicia just hadn't realized this would happen as early as the first grade.

"That's not such a bad name." And not far from the truth, Felicia thought.

Madeline exhaled a breath, blowing her bangs momentarily off her forehead. "I don't want him calling me that."

"Well, maybe you should try calling Jimmy by his name and he'll give you the same courtesy."

"I don't have to do what he says."

Yeah, spoiling adorable little Madeline might not be such a good idea. "No. You don't. But then he doesn't have to do what you say, either."

"That's why I'm not going to put his name on the rec board."

Okay, it was time to let Madeline know who the boss was, at least in this classroom. "You don't have that authority, Madeline. Only I can decide who goes on the board."

"I told you he called me a name," she said, her voice rising an octave.

Felicia remained calm. "And I've heard you call him names."

Madeline's pout grew, her impatience with Felicia showing. Felicia reached for the little girl's hand. "How about you help pass out the phonics books for this afternoon and leave the rec board to me?"

Madeline took a few minutes to consider Felicia's offer. Then, with a tentative smile, she slipped her tiny hand into Felicia's. With a smile, Felicia led the girl over to the bookstand. It wasn't a permanent solution to the problem of name-calling, but at least she'd avoided the all-out war that would have undoubtedly kicked off after Jimmy noticed his name intentionally left off the board, cutting him out of his recreational time.

As the two of them worked, Felicia thought again about the child growing inside of her and the man who was her husband. How would they raise their child? How would they draw the line between loving and spoiling this precious little miracle? She didn't have a clue, but she knew one thing for sure—she was going to love this baby unconditionally. It was a part of her and Ty—that alone was special. And maybe, just maybe, there would be more children for them on the horizon.

Chapter 4

After a brief visit with his mother, Ty had gone straight to the garage. His baby was there in all its shining glory. The teal exterior was spotless, and when he opened the driver's-side door and slid into the seat, he almost purred as the soft white leather greeted him. It had been much too long since he'd put her on the open road and pushed her to her limits.

Today was the perfect afternoon to do so. After starting the engine and backing out, he drove slowly, letting her warm up, down the winding driveway of the big house. His fingers gripped the steering wheel casually as his gaze roamed over the land that had once belonged to Harmon Braddock.

Rolling hills formed the acres that made up the Braddock estate. There was a guesthouse down on the eastern side of the property; just beyond was the golf course. To the west were the pool and tennis courts. And just behind the house was the garden his mother cherished as much as her time with her charities.

That brought to mind his and Malcolm's conversation with Evelyn Braddock a few hours earlier at the family estate.

"How are you dealing with everything?" Malcolm had asked.

"I'm holding up as well as can be expected," Evelyn had answered.

"You're a lot stronger than the rest of us," Malcolm had said as he sat on the sofa in the family room.

"Every day I wake up I think I miss him more," she'd said. "But he's gone and I'm still here. I have to finish living my life."

"We know," Ty had chimed in. "And we want you to know that we're here if on one of those mornings you feel a little too overwhelmed."

She eyed him carefully. "I'm a Braddock. I don't get overwhelmed. I cope."

"We're just offering our help, Mom. Just trying to let you know that you're not alone. We're coping, too," Malcolm said.

"I know, and I'm proud of the way all of you are handling things. It's important that families stand strong and together at times like this."

Ty had agreed, yet he'd come away from that visit still worried about his mother. On the exterior she seemed polished and perfect, just like his prized car. But Ty wasn't quite convinced. And from the concerned glance Malcolm had discreetly passed his way, neither was he.

Harmon's death was weighing heavily on her, as he guessed it would for anyone who lost a spouse. He didn't really know how he was supposed to help her, especially since she acted as if she needed no help at all. Passing the last bend before the road opened up like welcome arms, he'd tried to put it out of his mind. Nothing any of them did from this point on was going to bring his father back. It was best they all kept that little piece of reality in mind.

Now his foot eased down on the gas petal, and he felt his heart lurch with the power of the engine. This car could go zero to one-twenty in under sixty seconds, but he wasn't going to push her that fast, not today. Today he was looking for a mediocre amount of speed, enough so that his mind could be allowed free rein to think of how his life was changing.

Felicia was back in his life and she was pregnant. There weren't any words that could accurately describe how good that made Ty feel. His plan for adding children to his family didn't call for the blessed event to take place for another five years, but as he'd laid in his bed last night, he thought that was okay. She was carrying his baby now and she was giving him a second chance to be what she needed. Ty vowed to do just that.

And despite what Malcolm said, Ty knew he could please his wife and run his business. It was simply a matter of balance. His father had told him that, just before he'd run for Congress. Harmon Braddock had found his balance with work and family life. He'd been there for his children while building a career. And he'd instilled those same values in his son.

Peeping at his watch, Ty realized he'd been driving for more than an hour. It was close to three now, and there were still some things he needed to do at the office. He was working on a business deal that needed a lot of his attention.

Brentwood Industries owned a sporting goods conglomerate, Brentwood Sports. Since Ty and TJB Investments, through the TJB Global Fund, the hedge fund he'd opened on his own three years ago, invested primarily in retail entities, Brentwood would be just another feather in his cap. But Christopher Brentwood was a smooth character. Ty was definitely going to have to come at the older man with his A game to prove that, while he was young, he knew what he was doing.

Taking a hand from the wheel, he retrieved his cell phone and called his assistant, Marsha.

"Get Brentwood on the phone and see how soon we can meet. Sometime this week, preferably. I don't care what day or what time, just nail something down," he said as he circled the car around to head back to his parents' estate.

"Yes, sir," Marsha replied. "Mrs. Braddock called."

This announcement brought a smile to Ty's face. When was the last time Felicia had called him at work? "And?"

"She wanted to thank you for the flowers and said for you to call her later."

"Thanks, Marsha." Ty disconnected the call and continued to smile. He'd been thinking of Felicia the moment he'd awakened this morning, so calling to order her flowers had come naturally.

She wanted to be romanced and courted like she had in the beginning. He planned to overwhelm her with flowers and sweet gestures until she had no choice but to come back to their home. As with the business deal with Brentwood, there was no room for negotiating Ty's bottom line.

The day had been long, but thoughts of Ty had kept Felicia going. She wondered if she'd see him tonight. That was probably too optimistic, seeing as he'd given her all last night. However, the two dozen peach-colored calla lilies he'd had delivered to her this morning said he was at least thinking about her while he was at work. Of course, when she'd called, he'd been out at a meeting. She'd contemplated calling him on his cell but decided against it.

They'd been separated for months, and yesterday had been pretty emotional for both of them. Although, to his credit, Ty seemed to take the news of the pregnancy a lot better than she would have anticipated. If she wasn't mistaken, he actually looked pleased by the notion that they would be starting a family.

A family, she thought as she walked down the steps leading out of the school. She didn't want to live in the city anymore. The penthouse was too small for a family. Their child would need a yard for a swing, grass to roll and play on. Ty loved their penthouse in the city. Would he be open to moving? Funny how the doubts continued to surface. As much as she wanted to believe that they had a chance, that Ty could be the man she needed him to be, doubts still prickled her mind.

She was tired and hungry and sleepy. The first trimester of pregnancy was more than she'd anticipated. Her emotions were out of whack, her energy level had reached an all-time low and she was uncomfortable for the duration of the time she wasn't nauseous or worried. Her mother, who in addition to her father were the only other people who knew about the pregnancy, assured her that this was all the norm. In another couple of weeks, a lot of those symptoms would pass and she'd be on to other issues, like swollen ankles and growing pressure on her bladder.

She was thinking that she'd gladly endure all of this to stare into the eyes of her and Ty's child at the end of nine months, when a car horn caught her attention. She looked up then and noticed the sleek black Mercedes Maybach 62 S sedan. She would recognize that car anywhere because there weren't many people rich enough in Houston to own one. It was Ty's. Well, it was one of Ty's. That man loved his cars.

This one was for his driver, Deuce, whom he used when he was in the city. Ty's other cars, according to him, needed the open road to test their speed, so driving in the city wasn't logical. Instead, he had Deuce drive him to and from work and any other meetings he had in the city, or simply to the Braddock estate where he could pick up one of his other cars.

Her heart danced a little jig as she walked closer, her smile growing with each step. There was a small letdown when Deuce came around to open the back door for her and she realized Ty wasn't in the car.

"Good evening, Mrs. Braddock," Deuce said with his ready smile and deep dimples.

"Hi, Deuce," she said, coming up on tiptoe to kiss his weathered cheek. Deuce was a big man, with dark caramel skin, laughing eyes, a bald head and two huge hoop earrings in each ear. "It's good to see you."

"It's good to see you, ma'am. It's been far too long," he said, taking her bags from her arm and helping her into the car.

When she was settled, she waited for him to get in and asked, "Where's Ty and where are we going?"

Deuce only turned to her and smiled. "Just relax. Mr. Braddock told me to take good care of you. There's some cold water and fruit juice back there and something for you to snack on during the ride."

Felicia sat back against the pearl-gray bucket

leather seat, knowing it was pointless to ask Deuce anything else. The man was nothing if not loyal, and he'd been with Ty for years, so if Ty told him not to tell her where they were going, he'd walk on nails before divulging the information. She smiled as she slid forward in the seat to the minibar mounted on the back of the front seat. Picking up a bottle of orange juice, she surveyed the array of snacks and selected the caramel popcorn. She'd always had a sweet tooth and preferred that to the rice cakes and granola.

The ride shouldn't be too long, Felicia thought. Still, after her snack, she sat back in the seat and quickly fell asleep. When she awoke, it was to someone shaking her gently by the shoulders. Which probably wasn't a good thing to do since her stomach was rebelling against the popcorn and orange juice.

"Wake up, sleepyhead," Ty whispered against her ear.

When had he arrived? He must have been waiting for her at whatever their destination was. His voice registered and she struggled to lift her lids. When she'd finally closed them, sleep took her deeply so that it was a chore to wake up. "Hmmm." She tilted her head just a bit and was pleased to meet his lips.

The kiss was gentle, just a brushing of lips, but

it stirred her blood just the same and she lifted her arms to drape over his shoulders. "Hi," she said dreamily then pressed her mouth to his again.

"Mmm, hello yourself," Ty said, rubbing a thumb across her cheek. "You fell asleep on that short ride from the school to here."

"Where's here?" she asked groggily.

"We're at the Galleria. I thought you might like to do a little shopping and get some dinner."

He was staring at her as if he hadn't seen her in a very long time.

"Shopping?" she asked, trying to sit up. He was leaning over the console and he backed away a little while she got herself situated upright. "You hate shopping."

"I don't hate it," he said with a smirk. "I just don't see why somebody else can't do it for you."

"You were not brought up to be that uppity. Ms. Evelyn only has housekeepers because your father insisted and because Sarona is too ornery to leave. Otherwise she would still be scrubbing her own floors." She reached for her purse, opening it to grab her compact. If she looked like she felt, there was no way she was walking around in public without a little patchwork.

"And Ms. Lydia didn't bring you up to be so vain," he said, reaching for her compact.

She moved it out of his reach and lifted the sponge to dab concealer beneath her eyes. "I look like I haven't slept in ages. My mother would have a fit if I went out in public like this." Finished with the concealer, she pulled out her lip gloss and swiped the stick over her lips. "It's not for glamour, but for normalcy. You have no idea all the changes pregnant women go through."

Ty nodded. "Are you sick much? My secretary says she was ill the entire pregnancy."

Felicia's head snapped in his direction. "You told your secretary about the baby?"

Ty blinked as if confused. "Of course I did. Why? Is it a secret?"

"No," she said, shaking her head. "I just didn't think we were announcing it yet."

"Well, I didn't really announce it. I mean, nobody in the family knows, except Malcolm. I figured we could tell the others after church on Sunday."

Felicia had forgotten about the Sundays she and Ty had attended church with his parents. It seemed so long ago. "Oh." Unsure of what to say next, she placed all her things back in her purse and zipped it shut. His fingers gripped her wrists and her gaze was jerked back to his.

"You're beautiful without lipstick and whatever that other stuff was."

She smiled. "You're biased."

"I love you."

Deuce, as astute as always, picked that moment to open the car door. "If you're ready now," he said and reached inside to take Felicia's hand.

She gave it to him and stepped out into the slightly cooler evening air. Ty stepped out of the car behind her, reaching for her hand the moment he was at her side. "If you're too tired, we can just go home."

Home.

How badly she wanted to call the penthouse her home, with him, again. But she wasn't ready for that yet.

"No. I'll be fine. The walking is good for me, and you did interrupt my shopping yesterday."

They hadn't bought much, just half of the furniture for the nursery in Neiman Marcus and, because they didn't know the sex of the baby yet, a couple bags of basic baby wear. Felicia hadn't intended to get much as it was still early in the pregnancy. Some believed it was bad luck to shop too soon. However, Ty was convinced that their lives were changing for the better and wanted to buy whatever she liked.

Her feet were hurting a bit and she was hungry. Ty must have noticed she was getting tired because he chose a quick dinner over a fancy restaurant. They were back in the car after only two and a half hours.

"Let's get you home to bed," he said once she was fastened in with the seat belt.

That sounded like a great idea to her.

Ty watched her in awe as she let her head rest on the back of the seat. She was, just as he'd said, beautiful. More beautiful than he'd ever remembered seeing her. It must have been that baby glow his secretary was telling him about. When he'd planned this evening, he'd wanted to buy anything and everything that would make her smile. Instead, she'd smiled even before they'd gotten into the mall.

That was one of the things he loved about Felicia. She'd never been impressed by material things. Her wants were basic, her needs obtainable. On paper it seemed he was more than capable of pleasing her. But he wanted to do so much more than that. He wanted to take care of her, to make it so that there was never anything that she wanted or needed.

She was tired now, barely keeping her eyes open. As he'd been about to direct Deuce to take her to the penthouse, she'd given him an address just at the city limits. She'd not only moved out, she'd moved a good distance away from him.

Ty refused to think of that now. This evening had been good. They had been together and things seemed to be on the right path. He wouldn't let anything stop that.

He walked her to her door, noting that the apartment building was not the best. Felicia was in no way out of money. Even leaving him, she would still be comfortable financially. So the apartment wasn't the worst, but it wasn't good enough for her.

He couldn't hold his thoughts in any longer. "Why don't we just get your stuff and head back to the penthouse?" he said.

She'd unlocked the door and was just stepping inside when she glanced at him over her shoulder. "I like it here," she said. "For now."

The furniture, he noted as she turned on the lights, was in her customary style of "less is more." Not big pieces but the necessities. A couch, a recliner, a coffee table, a television stand. She had plants all around because she loved flowers and taking care of things that way. On a table in the corner, she had stacks of books, another one of her great loves. Felicia read anything and everything, all the time. He'd met her coming from the library, and since that time he could personally vouch for her having read over a million books.

"I'm going to get ready for bed, Ty. I have to get up early in the morning," she said, breaking his study of her apartment.

"How long are you planning to work?" he asked.

"As long as I can."

Ty nodded, her answer being what he'd expected to hear. "And how long do you plan on staying away from me?"

"I'm not staying away from you. We just spent another pleasant evening together. One I have to admit I am surprised by."

"Surprised? Why?"

"You haven't had a lot of evenings for me in a long while, Ty."

He nodded. "I know. Things have been hectic."

"So you said."

"I'm trying, Felicia," he said when it seemed like their conversation was headed down the wrong path.

She stepped to him, placing her hands on his shoulders. "I know you are, and that's all I can ask."

He cupped her face in his hands. "You can ask me for anything, Felicia. You've always had that power over me. Whatever I can do to make things right between us, I will do." He pulled her closer and rubbed his cheek against the top of her head.

"Just pay attention. That's all I ask," she whispered.

Because he loved the feel of her in his arms and because his baser needs for her were growing out of control, Ty lifted her face to his, dropping his lips down to hers, taking her mouth hungrily.

She opened to him willingly, stroking her tongue over his with need to match his own. The kiss grew deeper instantaneously, his hands raking through her hair as hers twined tightly around his neck.

Before he could stop himself, he was backing her toward the couch. When her legs hit the target, he lowered her down, covering her body with his own. He found her lips again, his teeth nipping along their line, his tongue seeking and tangling with hers.

They were so perfectly in sync, so one with their needs, that Ty had always been amazed. Felicia hadn't been as outgoing and extroverted as many of the girls they'd gone to school with, but she was well-known and liked for her quiet demeanor and pretty smile. Ty had figured there was more to her than what everyone was seeing. And he'd found it. He'd tapped into that sensual woman that could drive him wild with one kiss.

His body roared with need, blood thrumming through his system to rest painfully at his groin. As if she sensed his desire, her legs spread as much as could be allowed on the couch and he slipped between them. Rubbing his erection against her mound was like icing on the cake; hearing her moan his name, like heaven.

Cupping her breasts in his palms was another act he'd cherished. Felicia was petite but curved in all the right places. Her breasts, which used to fit perfectly in his palms, now overflowed with heaviness. He thrust between her legs again, wanting, needing to be inside of her quickly.

Beneath him she was panting, her head turning from side to side on one of the couch pillows. He loved when she was hungry for him, when she begged him to make her scream. She was holding on to that request, he could tell. She wanted to be stronger, to tell him to go and feel like she'd conquered some personal rule she'd made for herself. But Ty wanted something else.

The buttons on her shirt popped as he pulled the material apart. Her breasts, just as he'd felt in his hands, fairly exploded from her bra. They were so round and so full that his mouth watered simply at the sight. With shaking fingers, he thanked God for the front clasp on her bra and released it. Now that they were free, there was no reason why his mouth couldn't feast on those delicious mounds. Her areolas were huge and dark and round and his arousal grew harder than he thought he could stand.

"Ty," she moaned and arched, offering herself to him.

"Damn," was all he could manage to say before

grasping both breasts, bending his head and taking one stiff nipple between his teeth. She hissed then cursed, and every muscle in his body tightened.

"What's the matter? Did I hurt you?"

Looking down at her, Ty watched as she bit her bottom lip, her eyes closed so tightly he thought he'd have to physically help her reopen them. Ty quickly shifted his weight, wondering if he'd been too heavy on her stomach, on their baby.

"Felicia, sweetheart. Talk to me. Are you hurt?"

"It's okay," she said finally and reached up to touch a hand to his shoulder. "I'm fine."

"What did I do?"

"It's just another pregnancy symptom."

"What?"

"My…ah…my nipples are really sore. They say the tenderness will go away in a few weeks. I guess I hadn't realized how sore they were until you touched them. It's not like I've been touching them myself and—"

"And if you even say something that remotely sounds like another man's been touching them, I'm not going to be responsible for my actions," he said, moving so that he was sitting up and her feet were in his lap.

Felicia shifted, too, pulling her shirt over her exposed breasts as she did. "I wasn't going to say anything like that. Did you think I forgot how possessive you are?"

Ty shook his head. "Possessive is what a boyfriend is. I'm your husband. The thought of another man touching you makes me deadly."

"I would never cheat on you, Ty. Even though we were separated, we were still married. I took our vows very seriously."

He looked at her, saw how intense she'd just gotten. "Past tense? You're not still committed to us?"

She took a deep breath. "I wanted to be. I tried to be. But—"

Ty took her hands. "Okay, I see the need to reassure you is imperative in making this work. I apologize for not being there as much as you needed me to be and I am going to honestly work at changing that. I love you and I want you…I want us," he said, dropping a hand to her stomach. "I want us to be together. To be a family."

Tears glistened in her eyes as she said, "I want that, too."

"Then that's what we'll have. I told you when we first got married that I'd take care of you and I will. Just give me the chance."

He leaned forward and kissed her again, and like clockwork the kiss deepened. His hands were touching her breasts, much softer than he had before, and she was making that sweet little sound she did when she was close to erupting.

The room filled with a series of chimes. Felicia jumped and Ty sighed against her mouth. "It's my cell."

"Oh," she said, putting a hand to her chest as it chimed again. "Do you need to answer it?"

For a minute, Ty contemplated. He reached into his pocket and pulled out the phone. Glancing down at the number, he saw that it was Brentwood. It was almost nine at night, and the investor he wanted on board with him as badly as he wanted to make love to his wife was calling.

"Yeah," he answered tightly. "I'll just be a minute."

As Ty took the call, Felicia felt like she'd stepped under a cool spray of water. Just like that, their mood, the moment of intimacy that they hadn't shared in so long, had been interrupted by a business call.

She didn't have to see the number or hear him say it was business, she just knew. Ty was predictable that way. If it were family he'd have let them go to voice mail, then listen to the message to see if it was an emergency. If it were a stranger, he would have cursed and thrown the phone across the room. But he'd looked at the number and recognized it. He'd gotten that controlled, focused look in his eyes and he'd taken the call. It was business.

Getting up from the couch, Felicia went into her bedroom. She discarded the shirt that was now of no use to her and riffled through her drawer for a nightgown. She pulled it over her head then stripped off her pants and her shoes. Grabbing her unruly hair into a bundle, she stretched a band around it and looked for her slippers. She found them and returned to the living room, where Ty was just closing his phone.

He turned to her with a puzzled look on his face, clearly not getting her change of attire.

"I'm tired, Ty. I'm going to bed," she announced in a voice that was much more stable than she was feeling.

Ty walked to her, grabbed her around her waist and pulled her close to him. "I'd planned on putting you to bed."

And she probably would have let him, but she now knew in her mind it was too soon. Too soon to jump back into bed with him, to move back into the penthouse, to pick up where they left off. Her leaving him would have all been for nothing if she did. The phone call had brought those facts home.

"That's probably not a good idea just yet."

He frowned. "Is that sore, too?"

It took her a moment to figure out what he was talking about, and when she did, she slapped playfully at his chest. "No, silly. It's not a good idea because we're taking this reconciliation slowly."

"Sweetheart," he groaned as he pulled her closer to him so there was no doubt she felt his desire. "I need you."

"I need to get to bed," she said, although her body was screaming, *Take me now!*

Pulling back from her, Ty gave her a look that reminded her just how sexy he was. His butter-toned complexion and dark goatee made him look distinguished and important. The eyes that could be cutthroat and menacing in business were also warm and compassionate at home. "You sure I can't convince you?" he asked, licking his full bottom lip.

She moved out of his grasp to the front door, opening it for him. "I'm positive. Good night, Ty."

"All right," he said when he stood in the doorway. He turned back to grab her around her waist. "But you can't run forever."

Felicia had to smile. "That line worked when we were in college. We've been married for five years and it's not going to work now. We'll reunite in that way when the time is right."

His hand moved lower to cup her bottom. "You know how convincing I can be."

"And you know how stubborn I can be."

He smiled wickedly. "You won't last a week."

Ty was fiercely competitive in all things. "And what do I get if I do?" she challenged.

He lifted a brow. "What do you want?"

"A house for me and my family," she answered simply.

Chapter 5

Two long weeks later, at 3:15 a.m., Ty's house phone rang. He rolled over, cursing before his arm stretched to reach the receiver. He hadn't been sleeping well, thanks to his beautiful wife and her insistence that they work their way up to making love again.

For all the money he had, as smart as he was and as charming as he believed he could be, she still wasn't giving in. Hell, she acted as if she were a virgin and he a horny wolf on the prowl. It was a sin and a shame to keep a man in this constant state of arousal.

He knew his voice was gruff and irritated as he answered, but at this point he didn't give a damn. "Hello?"

"Ty?"

Her voice was soft and sexy and brushed over his aching body like a long smooth feather. "Felicia?"

"I need you."

Ty jumped out of the bed so fast he banged his knee against the nightstand. "What? Sweetheart, are you okay?"

"Yes," she said slowly. "I just need you to do something for me."

Holding the phone against his ear with one hand, Ty's other hand went instinctively to his arousal. Please let her say it, please, if there is a God, let her say it. "Anything, sweetheart. You know that."

"I want some ice cream."

His hand stilled. His body froze. "Ice cream?"

"Mmm-hmm. Mint chocolate chip."

With a silent curse, he snatched his hand from his groin and pinched the bridge of his nose. "It's…" He paused and looked at his clock. "It's three in the morning and you want mint chocolate chip ice cream?"

Felicia was now eleven and a half weeks pregnant. The baby book he'd purchased the day

after he'd left her apartment—because after the
breast incident he'd wanted to know all the symptoms and side effects of pregnancy—said that
cravings were normal throughout the entire nine
months. He hadn't realized that this craving would
have no conscience for a man suffering from lack
of sex and trying to close a big business deal. This
would be so much easier if she were lying here
next to him making this request.

"Ty, are you still there?"

The sound of her voice, the memory of how
soft she was in the middle of the night when he
would roll over and reach for her, the fact that she
was carrying his child, had time and distance
melting away. "I'll be there in a few minutes."

Felicia opened the door before he had a chance
to knock. She was dressed in a Bugs Bunny nightshirt, the floppy ears falling over each of her
breasts. She was bare from her knees to her feet
and her hair was disheveled. Yet to him she'd never
been prettier.

"Mint chocolate chip," he said, smiling, as he
held the bag with the ice cream out toward her.

She smiled in return, taking the bag from him
with one hand then pulling him inside with the other.
He'd had to drive his Aston Martin V8 Vantage—

which, luckily, he had driven into the city for yearly maintenance yesterday—to her house, as he couldn't see waking up Deuce at this hour for an ice cream run. All the way over he'd tried to think of anything besides making love to her. But it was pointless; more often than not in the last two weeks he'd found himself thinking of her. Whether it was in a carnal way or just about her smile, the sound of her laughter, or how good it felt to be with her in those evenings that he'd made a concerted effort not to work. She was always on his mind.

He closed and locked the door behind them, giving in and watching the sway of her very round, very delectable bottom in the short nightshirt. He'd thrown on some sweatpants and a sweatshirt, and his tennis shoes, and left the house, so his sex was free to move about at will. Which it was currently as he watched her walk across the room.

She didn't stop in the living room, as he'd thought she would, but continued back to her bedroom. "Can I get you anything else?" he asked.

"Yeah, come watch television with me," she said without stopping to see if he would follow her or not.

Of course he did. He sat tentatively on the side of her queen-sized bed as she got under the covers and took her ice cream from the bag.

"There's a spoon and some napkins in there,

too," he told her without turning around. He couldn't look at Felicia under the covers and surrounded by pillows without wanting to get under there with her. If she wanted him to watch television with her until she fell asleep, he would, but he'd stay as far away from her as he could in the process.

"Come up here and share it with me," she said and he heard her pulling the top off the container.

Ty groaned. "Felicia, sweetheart, you're killing me."

"What?"

"I'm trying to be a gentleman but you're not helping."

"I have no idea what you're talking about."

She was talking over a mouthful of ice cream when Ty risked it and turned to look at her. "When a man gets a call from a woman, his wife nonetheless, at three in the morning, it's not normally for ice cream. Then I get here and you barely have clothes on. You want me to sit in this bed and watch—" He glanced back at the television on the stand across the room. "You want me to watch some old black-and-white movie with you and get all cuddly in bed. I'm about to explode from sexual frustration and you ask me to do this."

For a moment she just stared at him. Then she smiled, scooping another spoonful of ice cream and extended her arm to him. "You forgot I offered to share my ice cream with you, too."

"Christ!" he growled and fell back on the bed, dropping an arm over his eyes.

"I called because I missed you," she said quietly, after a few moments of silence.

Ty sighed. He sat up, leaned over and took off his shoes. Standing, he removed his sweatshirt and sweatpants then climbed beneath the covers beside her. He lifted his arm and she snuggled closer to him. "I miss you, too." He kissed her forehead and let the feel of his wife in his arms, in bed, melt over him.

It had been too long. Missing her did not seem to accurately describe what he felt. He wondered if she had any idea how much he really loved her.

"So what's this we're watching?" he asked when she'd resumed eating her ice cream.

"The Women."

"That's a strange title for a movie." He looked at the screen, trying to see if he recognized any of the actors, and wasn't surprised that he couldn't.

"It's because there are no men in the cast."

"No men in the entire movie?"

She shook her head. "None."

"So what do the women do for an hour and a half?"

"Gossip, cheat on their husbands, file for divorce and then reconcile," Felicia said, counting off by tapping the spoon against the ice cream container.

Ty's heart clenched. "And you find that entertaining?"

She turned and looked up at him. "I find it hopeful. It proves that marriages gone bad can be good again."

Her words were so serious, her expression so stoic, Ty leaned forward and kissed the tip of her nose. "Our marriage *will* be good again."

Waking the next morning with Ty sleeping beside her had made the minor cramping in her back and the twisting in her stomach ease a bit. Felicia got out of bed slowly as the doctor had prescribed and made her way to the kitchen to get some crackers and a glass of water.

The craving for ice cream had been strong last night and had actually started earlier in the evening. But Ty had told her that morning when he'd called her at work that he had business meetings all day and wouldn't be able to stop by her place for dinner. She'd been distressed about that all day long.

He still has to work, she'd told herself over and over again. He couldn't spend every minute of every day with her, no matter how much she would have enjoyed it. These last couple of weeks with him had been blissful. Except for the fact that she came to her apartment at night and he went back to the penthouse, it was almost like a real marriage. Four out of the seven nights a week they were having dinner and spending the evening together, which was more than they had when she was living with him. He still talked about business, and she hadn't really expected him to stop. Managing his own hedge fund was a dream come true for Ty. Felicia shared his excitement; she simply wanted more of his time.

In the other room she heard his cell phone ringing and she sighed. It wasn't even seven o'clock yet and he was already working. Finishing off her water and then going to the bathroom, she tried not to think about it. He'd come when she'd called last night. He'd watched that movie with her and he'd held her while she slept. She wouldn't ask for anything more. Not today.

He was sitting on the edge of the bed when she entered the bedroom again. His cell phone was in his hand and he looked contemplative.

"Something wrong at the office?" she asked as

nonchalantly as possible. She then moved to her closet to find something to wear to work.

"That was Malcolm."

She turned to him. "Is everything okay? Evelyn's fine?"

"Mom's okay. At least she's acting like she's okay. She's going through the motions and functioning but there's this aura of sadness around her. I know it's to be expected, but it's still hard to watch."

"Losing your father was really hard on her. They were very close."

Ty nodded. "They were. After Dad took office he wasn't there as much, but Mom had other things to occupy her mind."

"All the committees and fund-raisers in the world don't take the place of having a husband," she said simply and watched as his gaze settled on her. Not today, she reminded herself. "So what did Malcolm want so early in the morning?"

"He needs to meet with me about something."

"That was cryptic," she said, then went back to her closet.

He came to stand behind her. "Wear the red shirt with those pants," he said. "I like you in red."

She turned to face him and frowned. "I don't think I can fit in the pants. I wore them the week before last and they were a little snug around my waist."

Ty tweaked her nose. "Sounds like you need to go shopping for maternity clothes."

He'd changed the subject, not wanting to tell her what was going on with him and Malcolm. To her relief, she knew that wasn't business. Malcolm was ambitious, but not in the moneymaking scheme of things. He had more civil goals in mind and, as she'd heard from Shondra, he was going to follow in Harmon's footsteps and run for office. "Yeah, I guess so."

When she would have turned back to her clothes, Ty held her still, hugging her tightly then pulling back enough to kiss her lips lightly. "Malcolm and I weren't talking business. There are some family things we're trying to tie up."

She sighed. "Is there something I can help with? I know I've been keeping my distance for a while but you know I love your mom and your family. If there's something I can do—"

He put a finger to her lips. "Shhh. I don't want you worrying about it. I'll handle it. You just take care of yourself and our baby. Okay?"

Felicia smiled, loving the feel of intimacy and normalcy they were sharing. Like a regular married couple about to get ready for work. "I can do that."

"Good. Now I've got to get back to the penthouse to change for work. Do you need anything before I go? Another pint of ice cream, some pickles? Maybe a hot pretzel with mustard?"

She laughed, pushing him away. "No. I don't have any cravings at the moment." She lied. She was craving *him*. How she'd managed to sleep beside him clad only in his boxers, she had no clue. But having him standing there, holding her, when his erection was so apparent, had warmed her all over. God, she wanted to push him back on that bed, lift her nightshirt and straddle him. It had been so long since she'd felt him inside her that some nights she'd debated calling him for just that reason.

"Hey, where'd you go just now?"

He'd given her a little shake. "Oh, I was just thinking of something."

"Of something or someone?"

"You are so arrogant," she said, smiling. "All right. I was thinking of you."

Ty hugged her again, pressing his arousal into her as he did. "Sweetheart, I want you, too. I don't know why you're putting us both through this."

She held on to him, for the first time in months feeling the depths of her love for this man. "I just want to be sure. I want it to work this time, Ty."

"Do you love me, Felicia?" he asked when he looked down at her.

"Yes. I do love you."

"Then that's all we need to make it work."

His words sounded so simple, so easy. So just like Ty to say.

TJB Investments, Inc., was located in downtown Houston. It was a large building, twenty-eight floors, including two restaurants on the lower level.

Ty loved the location and had rented an entire floor for his company. He had six associate finance advisors along with staff that handled the day-to-day operations of his holdings—namely the large retail chains that he owned until he was ready to either liquidate or sell them. The finance advisors didn't have their own accounts but worked to keep some of the clients abreast of their projects. Ty did the bulk of the research for new investors, as well as bringing in all new investments.

It was a demanding job, but one that Ty thrived at. To him, despite what his family thought, it was the thrill he got when the deal was closed. When he was able to acquire holdings, make his clients even more money and increase his own portfolio, he felt proud, accomplished. Like he was more than just Harmon Braddock's son.

Because he hadn't chosen to go into law like his father and like Shondra, he'd always felt he needed to work harder. He hadn't followed in Malcolm's and his mother's steps, either, taking up one cause or another and fighting for it.

He was the middle child with a different set of goals and dreams. He only hoped that he would at least take from his father the ability to juggle both a successful career and a family.

"Mr. Brentwood is camping with his family up at Lone Star this weekend. He's asking if you could meet him up there," Marsha said. She was in his office going over messages and his schedule for the day.

Ty had been distracted since arriving in the office this morning. Leaving Felicia had caused an ache in his chest he wasn't familiar with. As long as they had gone to their own places and slept in their own beds, he'd had a grip on this separation process. A slight grip, but one nonetheless. Now that he'd slept in the same bed with her again, it wasn't so easy to go back to the idea of sleeping alone.

"Mr. Braddock?" Marsha called his name with an edge of concern and placed her notepad on her lap.

"Yes?" He looked at her and rubbed a hand over his face. "I'm sorry, what were you saying?"

"Is everything all right, Mr. Braddock? I mean, with the baby and your wife?"

"Everything's fine. Why do you ask?"

"You look worried."

Ty tried to smile. Marsha had been with him since he'd started the TJB Fund. She was a good worker and tried to be a friend. More often than not, Ty brushed that off. Today, he thought he might need her in that regard. "I've been reading about pregnancy and everything that goes along with it. I'm just wondering what else I can do for Felicia at this point."

Marsha's features instantly turned from professionalism to compassion. "Is she getting enough rest? Plenty of water, eating right and rest is all she can do right now."

He leaned back in his chair, his gaze momentarily resting on his degrees and awards neatly framed and hanging on the wall. "She's still working and that bothers me."

"She's a schoolteacher, right? That shouldn't be too stressful. Her kids are still too young to give her too much trouble. Is there anything else going on at home? Any reason why you'd be worried about the pregnancy?"

Ty was not about to tell Marsha that he and Felicia were separated, no matter how helpful she was trying to be.

"I'm probably just being paranoid. She seems fine. All the normal symptoms of early pregnancy

are there. Right down to the cravings," he said
with a smile, remembering last night.

She smiled. "That's a good thing."

"Yeah." Ty thought about his wife for another
moment before adjusting himself in his chair and
clearing his throat. "Now back to business. Have
we heard from Brentwood today?"

Picking up her notepad again as if the conversation switch was the most natural in the world,
she replied, "As I was saying before, he called just
before you came in. He wants to meet with you
personally. Says all these conference calls and
e-mails aren't working for him. He needs to meet
with you in person before he can make a decision
as important as this."

Ty steepled his fingers and rested them on his
chin as he thought about her words. "Fine. Set up
a face-to-face." He hoped it wasn't in the man's
hometown of Lexington, Kentucky. Leaving Felicia right now was not going to go over well.
She'd never understand and would assume things
were back to the way they were before.

"He'll be in Texas this weekend. Camping up
at the Lone Star with his family. You could go up,
take Mrs. Braddock with you. Meet with Brentwood and get some R & R while you're at it."

Marsha was more perceptive than Ty had ever

given her credit for. A weekend away with Felicia would be great. A change of scenery in such a restful atmosphere would be good for her. Not to mention the uninterrupted time they'd get to spend together. "Make the arrangements for a cabin. Set up a time with Brentwood and get my wife on the phone," he said before lifting his cup of now-cold coffee to his lips.

He noticed the look of satisfaction on his secretary's face as she left his office. Less than a minute later she buzzed him. "Mrs. Braddock on line four."

"Thanks." Ty was smiling when he picked up the phone. "Hello, Mrs. Braddock. You miss me yet?"

He heard her chuckle on the other end and enjoyed the warmth that spread throughout his chest. "I just left you two hours ago."

"One hundred and twenty minutes is a long time."

"I agree. So you must be missing me to have called this soon."

"Missing you like crazy, sweetheart. Never doubt that," he said honestly. "Listen, I have an idea. How about you and I spend the weekend cuddled up, sort of like we did last night, in a cabin at Lone Star?" Ty just prayed that, unlike last night, this weekend would finally be the moment when Felicia gave in to both their desires.

"An entire weekend, just you and me?" she asked hesitantly.

Ty hated that questioning in her voice, like she was just waiting for the other shoe to drop. "Of course, just you and me. I'm not about to invite anyone else along to cuddle up with my wife."

She chuckled again. "You know what I mean, Ty. You're going to not work for an entire weekend? What about the big investor you're trying to snag?"

"Don't worry about that. I don't want you worrying about my work or your work or anything other than keeping yourself and our baby healthy. I just want to spend some alone time with you. You know when the baby comes we won't have much of that."

"That's true. In that case, I'd love to spend the weekend with you, Mr. Braddock."

"Great. We'll leave around noon on Friday. I have a meeting in the morning but that should be over by eleven. I'll pick you up and we can get right on the road. Lone Star's only an hour away."

"That sounds… Oh, no, wait. I can't."

For a moment, Ty was alarmed. "You can't. Why?"

"It's Halloween. The kids have a party Friday night at the school. I have to be there."

Sometimes, Felicia was as dedicated to her job as he was, so Ty couldn't fault her for that. "That's fine. How about I meet you at the party and we'll hit the road as soon as it's over?"

"That sounds like a plan."

"Great. I'll call you a little later and we'll talk about dinner tonight."

"Okay," she said. "Oh, and, Ty?"

"Yes, sweetheart?"

"I love you."

It was all worth it. All the changes he was making, all the work he was doing, everything he had planned. It was all worth hearing those words from Felicia and knowing she absolutely meant them. "I love you, too."

Chapter 6

Friday night couldn't have come sooner. Felicia had spent the past three days packing and trying not to think about how much she was going to enjoy this weekend. Three days alone with her husband. When was the last time she'd had that?

Deuce had come to her apartment that morning before she'd left for work to pick up her suitcase, so now all she had to do was get through the day at work and tonight's party.

The kids were very excited about the Halloween party they had been preparing for all week long. It was only the first- and second-graders, and they were all dressing in costumes. After the last bell of the day, the kids were going home and returning to the school in full costumes at six o'clock.

It was now five forty-five and everything was in place. Felicia adjusted the apron of her Alice in Wonderland costume as she headed down the hall to the gym to make one final check of the decorations. She'd stuffed her cell phone in the bodice of the outfit, since she didn't have any pockets. When it rang, she was a little alarmed, then laughed. The vibrating against her breasts had all sorts of sexual alarms going off in her body. This holding out from Ty was definitely coming to an end tonight. She was no saint and once a woman was Ty Braddock's lover, going abstinent was no walk in the park.

"Hello?"

"Hey, sweetheart. How about coming to the front door to let me in?"

"Ty? Where are you? The party hasn't even started yet."

"I know. That's why I'm here. How would it look, me showing up to a costume party once it was over?"

Ty did not do parties, and he definitely did not do children's parties. "But I thought you were going to pick me up afterward."

"As much as I love hearing your voice over the

phone, sweetheart, I'd much rather see your pretty face. Can you come and open the door?"

"Oh, yeah. Sure."

Turning in the opposite direction, Felicia walked quickly down one corridor then turned the corner, passed the main office and opened the front door. The kids would use the side entrance near the gym to get in. There were already a few teachers and aides there to receive them.

"Hey—" The words died on her lips when she looked at him. He was dressed in green scrubs and had a stethoscope hanging around his neck, and she couldn't help but giggle. "You dressed up?"

"So did you." He stepped through the door and touched the hair of her long blond wig.

She couldn't stop staring at him. His body looked tight and fit even in the loose outfit. But that wasn't the surprise. The surprise was that he was here, in her school, dressed as a doctor to attend her class's Halloween party. To say she was happy was an understatement.

"What's the matter? You've never seen such a sexy doctor?" he joked.

She wanted to smile. She wanted to cry. So many emotions were running through her right now she felt overwhelmed. "I'm, ah, just a little shocked, that's all."

He brushed a hand over her cheek. "I told you I would make things better between us. If it means dressing up and coming to an elementary school party, then that's what I'll do. Is that all right with you?"

Tears swam in her eyes as she tried to keep them from falling. "It's…ah…just fine with me."

"Don't cry, sweetheart. I don't want anything to mar your pretty face. Besides, it's a party. We should go enjoy ourselves." He took her hand. "Which way?"

"Down here." She pointed. "To the gym."

"You look really hot in that costume," he said as they neared the gym.

She laughed. "I'm a character from a children's cartoon. How hot is that?"

"Your breasts are too big for you to be considered a child, and that dress is barely covering your knees. I'm so aroused right now I'm liable to poke somebody's eye out, so you might want to keep close."

"Oh, don't worry, Mr. Braddock. I'm not about to let the sexiest doctor I've ever seen out of my sight. You'll be right by my side all night long." And for the rest of her life, Felicia hoped.

As they entered the gym, Ty leaned over and

whispered in her ear, "And what about tonight when we get to the cabin? Where will I be then?"

She looked up at him, knowing exactly where his mind was going and loving every minute of it. "You'll be inside of me, where you belong."

Felicia had taken a round of girls to the bathroom for the final time of the night. The party would be over in fifteen minutes. She was just headed back into the gym to find Ty when she spotted him across the room. There were only about twenty kids left, and the staff had already begun wrapping things up.

Ty was talking on his cell phone. Felicia took a deep breath to keep from getting angry about it. Hadn't he come dressed to her Halloween party? On top of that, he'd been amazing with the kids.

At one point during the night, Amanda Darson, a very shy little girl who was dressed as Cinderella, had been sitting all alone in a chair near the punch table. Ty had excused himself from Felicia and the group of teachers they were speaking to and went to sit next to her.

Felicia couldn't tell what he'd said to Amanda but after a few minutes she'd seen the little girl smile. In the next minute, Ty had taken her hand and led her to the dance floor. Felicia's heart practically leapt out of her chest as she watched Ty put Amanda's feet on top of his and dance her around the room. It was the sweetest thing she'd ever seen, and her hand had instantly gone to her stomach. Tyson Jamison Braddock was going to be a wonderful father. He was going to love this child she was carrying with all his heart. She had no doubt about that.

Ty closed his phone and walked toward her as she finished remembering the events of the night. That confident stride and self-assured attitude he possessed appealed to her more now than ever.

"Before you ask, I was talking to Shondra. Just letting her know where we'll be for the weekend in case they need to reach me. Sometimes you can lose connectivity in the wilderness."

Felicia could only smile, her heart overflowing with love for this man. She grabbed his hand, then told Lucy, her aide, to see the girls to their parents and continue with the pack-up, she'd be right back.

"Where are you taking me, Mrs. Braddock?" Ty asked when they continued to walk through the long halls.

"You've been a bad boy, Mr. Braddock."

"Really?" he asked from behind her. "Am I about to be punished?"

"You bet your green scrubs you are," she

quipped. They came to a room that she knew would be unlocked. She opened the door and pulled him inside. Before he could open his mouth to speak again, Felicia was on him, taking his mouth with all the hunger she'd held at bay these last few weeks. Ty didn't hesitate but snaked his arms around her back and pulled her closer to the hardness of his body.

Ty's doctor outfit left nothing to the imagination. Felicia moaned as his thick erection pressed into her. Shifting positions, Ty moved so that Felicia's back was now up against the door. Without a word, he lifted her legs. She obediently wrapped them around his waist. His hands slid under the dress she wore and slipped beneath her panties to touch the skin of her bottom. He gripped her there and took her mouth in another steamy kiss.

She was panting now, her body aching for him. "Ty," she whispered desperately when he'd left her lips to trail moist kisses along her jawline and down her neck. "I need you."

"Relax, sweetheart. I know what you need." He slipped one hand from behind her to her pulsing center.

The moment he touched her there, Felicia wanted to scream. Instead she bit her lip, letting her head fall against the door. It had been too long since he'd touched her like this. He slipped one finger inside, pulled it out, then slipped in two. She trembled and whispered his name. His fingers went deeper as his thumb pressed firmly over her already tightened nub.

Her thighs clenched around Ty's waist. He kissed her neck while working his magic between her legs. "How was I a bad boy?" he said before nipping her neck.

Felicia heard his words but couldn't summon a response.

"Come on, sweetheart. I need you to talk to me. You know how I like it."

And she did. Ty was a patient and kind lover; he only asked for one thing in return. He loved for her to talk to him.

"You haven't touched me like this in too long," she said finally.

He growled and pressed his fingers deeper inside her. "I wanted to."

"I wanted you to," she moaned. "Oh, God. I wanted you to touch me so badly."

"I can't wait to get you alone in that cabin."

"Oh, Ty," she whimpered. Her thighs began to quiver, her release humming along her very sensitive nerves.

"Yes, sweetheart. Let it flow." He pumped his

fingers into her again, holding her around her waist steadily with his other arm. "Let me take care of you right now. Then we can leave."

Felicia opened her mouth to speak but was silenced by the rush of her orgasm tearing through her body.

Her breathing was just returning to normal when Ty let her legs down. Thankfully he kept his arms around her until she was steady. Then she stood on tiptoe, placing a soft, lingering kiss on his lips. "And when we get to the cabin, I'm going to take care of you," she whispered against his mouth.

"Is that a promise?"

"That's a fact," she stated. Then she looked down to try and fix her clothes.

Ty peeked out of the closet to make sure nobody was in the hallway. "I told you it was a bad idea to wait," he joked.

"It was necessary," she said and tentatively stepped out of the closet behind him.

"It was crazy and you've been denying yourself all this time for nothing." Ty stopped just before they were back at the gym. Putting a finger to her chin, he tilted her head up and looked into her eyes. "But that game stops now. When we get to that cabin, you're going to forget all about this little trial period you've been giving us."

Felicia cleared her throat. "I am?"

He nodded. "Yes. You are. And I'm going to make love to you very thoroughly, very slowly, all night long."

She wanted to groan. Just the thought had her legs shaking again. "Then we'd better hurry up and get finished here. I don't think I can wait much longer."

Ty laughed. "You always were insatiable. I swear I don't know how you've held up all this time. That's why you dragged me into that closet."

Felicia was already moving to open the door when she chuckled. "That's why I needed all that ice cream—to cool myself down."

Chapter 7

It was almost midnight by the time Felicia and Ty got to the cabin.

She had never been a huge outdoor person and wasn't really looking forward to roughing it, so to speak. Luckily for her, the cabin had all the modern amenities. Ty had let her in, turning on the lights before leaving to retrieve their bags from the car.

While he was outside, Felicia walked around, the two-and-a-half-inch wedge heels of her boots echoing on the wooden floor. It smelled like a mixture of cedar and musk. The decor was rustic but charming. There was a huge living room with a fireplace on one wall and wide windows on the other. This room led to a corner with a dining table and four chairs. The kitchen was small but functional. Down a short hall, she could see two doors that she assumed led to the bathroom and bedroom.

It was cozy and romantic, Felicia thought as she heard Ty come through the door.

"Are you hungry?" he asked as he secured the latch lock on the door.

"Nope. Those hot dogs at the party filled me up."

Ty looked at her then shook his head.

"What?"

"Those hot dogs or the pumpkin Rice Krispie treats and marshmallow ghosts you kept taking when you thought I wasn't looking."

Felicia moved past him to grab her bag. "I don't know what you're talking about."

"Leave that alone," he said, swatting her hands away from the bag. "Go get your shower. I'll unpack."

"Are you sure you can trust me out of your sight? You're not afraid I might eat something else?" She crossed her arms over her chest and tried to look indignant.

"No. Because there's no food in the bathroom." He chuckled then blocked her as she swung at his gut.

"It's not funny. I *am* eating for two, you know."

"I know," he said, lifting the bags and walking behind her into the bedroom. "But maybe I'd like for my son to experience more than mint chocolate chip ice cream and Halloween snacks."

She turned on him so fast he dropped the bags just inside the doorway and prepared to block another attack.

Felicia stifled a grin. She wasn't going to swing on him again, but she was going to set him straight.

"Look," she said poking a finger into his shoulder. "*I'm* the one that's pregnant. *I'm* the one who's either hungry or nauseous every second of the day. *I* know how to eat and what to eat. And if I want sweets I'm going to have them. I'm not going to gorge on them only, but I'm not really in the mood to deny myself right now."

He took slow, measured steps toward her. Felicia wasn't sure she liked that look in his eyes so she backed up—until she backed into the wall.

Ty didn't stop his progression. Instead he reached forward and cupped her face in his hands.

"I'm not in the mood to deny you, either," he said. Then he traced his tongue along the line of her lips.

Trembling, her mind instantly went blank so that food was now the furthest thing from it. She opened her mouth, wanting the warmth of his tongue inside, but he moved to the left, kissing her cheek, the line of her jaw and down to her neck.

"Ty," she whispered, lifting her arms to wrap around his neck.

"Shower," he mumbled as one hand cupped her breast, his lips trailing a heated line over her collarbone. "Then I'm going to kiss every…inch… of…your…body." Those last words were punctuated by openmouthed kisses.

Her center pulsed, her body humming with sexual awareness. "I can't," she sighed. "Wait."

"Yeah. You can." He pulled away to gaze into her eyes. "Just like I waited. Burning with need for you every night. Thinking about you nonstop every day."

He reached down and cupped her mound through her jeans. Dammit, why had she changed from her fairy-tale dress? It would have offered easier access.

She writhed against his touch.

Oh yeah, she was good and hot. This was exactly how Ty wanted her.

Exercising the same patience he used when waiting for an investment to reach its peak, Ty pulled away from her.

She was about to protest when he touched a

finger to her lips. Her gaze burned into his, mirroring all the pent-up desire he'd felt these past weeks.

With unhurried fingers, he found the hem of her shirt and lifted it over her head. His throat tightened at the sight of her full breasts constricted in the black bra she wore. Grabbing her shoulders, he turned her around, found the clasp and released it. Tossing the bra across the floor he left her back facing him but cupped each mound until they overfilled his hands.

She gasped and relaxed back against him. When his erection was painfully pressing against his pants, Ty slid his hands down her torso, stopping at the bump that signified she was pregnant.

Felicia had always had a flat stomach, so this contrast was very noticeable. Ty let his hands linger, loving the knowledge that beyond his palms, his child grew inside this woman.

This woman that he'd loved for what seemed like all his life. His heart was so full of emotion he thought he would weep with it.

Instead he kissed her bared shoulder then moved his hands to the elastic band on her jeans. He'd already begun pushing them, along with her underwear, down past her hips when it dawned on him she still had her shoes on.

He picked her up and carried her to the bed.

Sitting her down on the edge, he quickly fell to his knees and removed her boots. Pulling her jeans and underwear completely off, Ty reached for her and pulled her to a standing position once more.

"My turn," she said and immediately reached for him.

Ty stepped out of her reach and said, "Wait."

He looked down at her feet, loving the daintily painted pink toenails. His gaze continued upward, past her calves to the splay of her hips and the neatly trimmed juncture between her legs.

Although his blood pumped with lust, his heart bled with emotion as he focused again on her stomach. In six months his child would be born into this world—into this circle of love between him and Felicia.

Her chest heaved under his blatant perusal. Her breasts were heavy and enticing, her nipples large and erect. He smoothed his tongue over his lips at the sight then hurriedly removed all his clothes.

Only when they were both standing naked did he reach for her again, lifting her into his arms and kissing her languidly.

He carried her into the bathroom, putting her down in the shower only after he'd managed to open the door to the stall and run the water for a few minutes until its temperature was appropriate.

She reached for him and he stepped in behind her, closing the door. The warm spray pelted both their bodies as their hands touched and roamed over each other's flesh. It was a reunion of sorts. Him reuniting with the feel of her and she doing the same. There weren't many words because, for as long as they'd been together, declarations seemed useless.

With his body burning with need, Ty quickly found the soap and lathered her body. After he rinsed her off, Felicia did the same for him. His ironclad control had slipped its final notch the moment she grabbed his length into her soapy hands.

He quickly had them both under the spray of water again then out the stall and headed to the bedroom. Once there, Ty paused long enough to dry her and himself off. Then he laid her on the bed, spreading her legs wide.

"Dammit," he mumbled as his fingers squeezed her thighs. He clenched his teeth then bowed his head, his tongue finally making contact with her plump nether lips.

She bucked beneath him. Ty rested his face in her juncture and inhaled deeply, letting her intoxicating scent invade him. With shaky fingers, he parted her lips then pressed his tongue inside.

"Ty. It's been so long," she whispered.

"Never again," he growled when he was able to pull his lips from hers. "Never again will I go this long without tasting you."

And then his mouth was on her again.

Seconds later she cried out his name as her second orgasm of the night overtook her. When her tremors had stopped, Ty moved upward, covering her body with his. He took her mouth, kissing her deeply. She loved to taste herself on his lips, and she showed her appreciation by reaching between their bodies to stroke his aching erection.

Without permission, Ty pumped into her hand, loving the expertise with which she handled him. When she gaped her legs and led his erection to her now-creamy core, he swore and let her take control.

She guided him slowly, pressing his tip against her entrance then going perfectly still. His gaze immediately shot to hers in question. For one exaggerated moment, he thought she was changing her mind.

"Never again," he whispered, then lifted her hips until another inch of him slipped inside.

Bringing her hands up, she cupped his face. "Never again will I go this long without you inside me."

On those words, Ty thrust his full length into her waiting heat. They both moaned at first, holding perfectly still as if capturing this moment in time.

Then their bodies took over, moving with familiarity, driving each of them to the phenomenal bliss that awaited.

Time seemed to stand still as he moved over her, burying himself deeper than he'd ever thought he'd gone before. She was so open, so wet and so accepting of him at this very moment that Ty's mind blurred with desire. His teeth clenched as he aimed for the exact spot that would make her shiver.

"Ty," she whispered, then gasped. Her thighs tightened around his waist and he knew he'd found the spot.

With another rotation of his hips, her nails were sinking into the skin of his shoulders, and Ty rode the wave of her climax, loving the clench of her walls and the drenching of her release surrounding him.

When it was his turn, he gently lifted Felicia, turning her over and grabbing a few pillows to place beneath her stomach. After ensuring that she was comfortable, Ty ran his hands along her now-elevated bottom, loving the soft feel of each globe. Spreading her thighs a little wider, he angled himself until the head of his arousal glided along the slickness of her center.

"God, I love you," he said through clenched teeth, closing and reopening his eyes to make sure he wasn't dreaming.

Pushing slowly into her, ever mindful of the deepness of this entry and the possibility of hurting her, he watched for any signs of discomfort.

"Ty, please," Felicia moaned.

Holding on was becoming next to impossible. His release was close, the tiny beating in the base of his spine clear evidence. "Please, what, sweetheart?"

He held still over her, waiting for her answer.

"Please…more…" she panted, undulating her hips in an attempt to take him farther inside.

Ty almost exploded right then and there. "Yes," he said tightly. "More." He pushed into her, still slowly, but undoubtedly. "More." He pulled almost completely out before sinking back into the heated cove. "More."

His rhythm picked up until he was riding her in earnest. The room filled with her yelling his name and him promising to love her this way for all time.

Release came on a tidal wave of heat, thrusting Ty into a sphere he'd never known existed as he emptied all of himself into her.

He was hers completely; that fact had never been far from his mind. She could make or break him with a word, and that frightened him. He couldn't…no, he wouldn't lose her, ever. That was no longer a promise, but now a pledge.

* * *

Felicia had no idea what time it was when she awoke the next morning.

But she was alone.

She was about to call Ty, thinking he was just in another room, but her stomach did what was now its routine churning and she quickly got out of bed.

Twenty minutes later, her stomach was officially empty. She brushed her teeth and washed her face before heading toward the kitchen barefoot.

"Thank God," she sighed when she opened the cabinets to find them full of food.

She still wasn't sure what time it was exactly, but it must have been late morning, like after ten. She normally ate breakfast around eight with a snack at ten. Eating several small meals a day seemed to help alleviate her nausea. If she woke up sick, she must have missed her morning repast.

Looking around the room, as if on second thought, Felicia realized Ty wasn't in there, either. She put on a pot of water for tea then leaned against the counter, arms folded over her chest, trying like hell to convince herself that her husband could not be out doing business in the wilderness.

The door opened and her gaze flew in that direction.

"You finally made it out of bed?" Ty asked,

stepping inside and closing the door with his foot. His arms were full of firewood.

"What time is it?" Felicia asked, trying not to sound as conflicted as she felt.

"Almost noon," he said. He moved to the fireplace and piled the wood into a neat stack. "Have you eaten?"

He was walking toward her now, wearing jeans and a button-down black shirt. His Timberland boots looked brand-new. Ty didn't dress down often. Felicia wasn't the least bit shocked that he looked as scrumptious in casual wear as he did in designer suits.

"I was just going to try some tea."

He cupped her face in his hands and dropped a soft kiss on her lips. "Sit down. I'll fix you something."

Felicia blinked. "*You?* Fix *me* something?"

"Is there a problem with that? I'm going to get offended if you keep doubting my culinary skills." Ty pulled out one of the wood-backed chairs at the table and made sure she sat.

"No problem at all, Mr. Braddock."

"Good, because I've gathered some skills since you've been away. However, I still keep Sarona very busy."

Felicia grinned. "I'm sure you do."

* * *

An hour later, after a very tasty ham-and-cheese omelet, Felicia had showered and dressed and was slipping on a lightweight jacket as Ty held the front door open for her.

Stepping outside into the fresh smell of outdoors she zipped her jacket and looked around. "So how far is this surprise you want to show me?"

"It's not too far," he said, coming to stand beside her and taking her hand in his. "Besides, exercise is good for the baby."

"I know that and I have no problem with walking. It's the wilderness I'm worried about."

Ty chuckled. "You'll be fine. There's nothing out here to hurt you."

"Yeah? How many times have you traipsed around the forest?"

"Not many. But we're going to stick to this trail and loop around until we're back at the cabin. It'll be nice."

Felicia shrugged. "If you say so."

They walked in companionable silence, their booted feet cracking twigs and already dry leaves on the ground. Though she considered herself a city girl, she was starting to appreciate the beauty of the outdoors.

Trees stretched until their tops seemed to brush

IMANI
ROMANCE

An Important Message from the Publisher

Dear Reader,

Because you've chosen to read one of our fine novels, I'd like to say "thank you"! And, as a special way to say thank you, I'm offering to send you two more Kimani Romance novels and two surprise gifts – absolutely FREE! These books will keep it real with true-to-life African American characters that turn up the heat and sizzle with passion.

Please enjoy the free books and gifts with our compliments...

Linda Gill

Publisher, Kimani Press

Peel off Seal and Place Inside...

FREE GIFT
PUBLISHERS
SEAL
THANK YOU

THE EDITOR'S "THANK YOU" FREE GIFTS INCLUDE:

▶ Two NEW Kimani Romance™ Novels
▶ Two exciting surprise gifts

YES! I have placed my Editor's "thank you" Free Gifts seal in the space provided at right. Please send me 2 FREE books, and my 2 FREE Mystery Gifts. I understand that I am under no obligation to purchase anything further, as explained on the back of this card.

PLACE FREE GIFTS SEAL HERE

168 XDL ERR5   368 XDL ERSH

FIRST NAME	LAST NAME

ADDRESS

APT.#	CITY

STATE/ PROV.	ZIP/POSTAL CODE

Thank You!

The Reader Service — Here's How It Works:

If offer card is missing write to: The Reader Service, 3010 Walden Ave., P.O. Box 1867, Buffalo, NY 14240-1867

BUSINESS REPLY MAIL

FIRST-CLASS MAIL   PERMIT NO. 717   BUFFALO, NY

POSTAGE WILL BE PAID BY ADDRESSEE

THE READER SERVICE
3010 WALDEN AVE
PO BOX 1867
BUFFALO NY 14240-9952

NO POSTAGE
NECESSARY
IF MAILED
IN THE
UNITED STATES

the pale blue sky. The area wasn't dense; sunlight filtered through as if artistically captured in a painting. And the company couldn't be beat.

He still held her hand but walked ahead of her so that she viewed his back as they trekked along. His shoulders were broad and pronounced under his jacket. She almost forgot how well-built he was. He must still be working out.

A short while later, the tree cover began to break, showing more sky and sunlight than before. Ty slowed down.

"It's just down here," he said, guiding her down a short incline.

Felicia was about to ask another question when she saw it.

As if this section of the forest had not been touched by the crisp fingers of fall, the grass was a brilliant green. The stream trickled over boulders that stretched up out of the earth in magnificent splendor.

The clearing had no trees but more ambiance than anything else she'd seen on this makeshift hike yet.

"It's beautiful." She sighed.

He released her hand as she admired the surroundings and stood behind her. His arms snaked around her waist, pulling her back against him.

"That's what I said when I saw it this morning."

"What time did you get up?"

"Around six. I never was a late sleeper."

"I remember," she said softly.

They stood quietly, watching the water and the infrequent burst of birds streaking through the sky above. This was peaceful and more relaxing than the nap she'd been thinking about taking when they returned to the cabin. And it seemed like the perfect spot. Like she and Ty belonged here, together at this moment.

"I hope she has your thirst for knowledge," Ty said suddenly.

"Who?"

"The baby."

"You think it's a she?"

She felt him shrug behind her. "If it's a she, I hope she's just like you."

Felicia smiled. "And just like you if it's a boy?"

"Not *just* like me. I hope he has your heart and your courage, as well."

Felicia turned in his arms. "I want him to have your sense of loyalty and dedication. And your business sense."

Ty frowned and Felicia was instantly worried she'd said something wrong.

"He doesn't have to be in the business I'm in. I don't even want him to feel pressured about that."

"Is that how you feel? Pressured to be a business-man?" She watched as a muscle in his jaw clenched.

"I've always felt compelled to succeed. At times it's been a very heavy burden. One I don't want my son to carry."

"Harmon didn't seem like the type of father to put pressure on you."

"No. He didn't verbally. It was just known." Ty moved away, getting closer to the stream. "Brad-docks did not fail. He'd been a successful D.A., then he led a successful campaign and became a congressman. He did great work for his constitu-ents and his family. It was a tough act to follow from the get-go."

"Nobody said you had to follow him."

"It didn't have to be said. It was implied. Mal-colm went to college and he went to law school. Up until a year ago, he'd done everything my father wanted him to do. I, as the second son, the middle child, could afford to do no less. I had my own goals but I felt as if I had to make them as high as my father's so that I'd at least meet him on that level." He shook his head. "You couldn't under-stand the pressure I felt and still feel."

"But is it pressure that you bring on yourself?" Felicia asked tentatively. "I know I came in as the outsider, but all I ever saw was Harmon's undying love for his family. He and your mother seemed to have wanted the best for you and Malcolm and Shondra, whatever that was."

"You're right, you were looking in from the outside."

Felicia's heart ached for the turmoil she could see on Ty's face. How had she managed to be married to him for so long and not realize how a large part of him was unhappy? Now, ten years later, he was finally opening up, showing her a side of him she would have never guessed existed.

If there was one thing she knew for certain about Ty, it was that failure, in his eyes, was an abominable sin. If Ty was carrying guilt over somehow letting Harmon down and not being able to reconcile it before Harmon died, then it was definitely eating him up inside. In that moment she pitied the boy who feared he'd disappointed his father, but still loved the man who would push on regardless.

"I think Harmon was very proud of the man you became, Ty. Regardless of what path you took to get there."

Ty didn't speak, so Felicia wrapped her arms around his waist, laying her cheek against his back. "I've always been proud of the man you became."

He lifted his hands to cover hers. "I've always

loved you, Felicia. At first, my desire to succeed was rooted in my father and proving myself to him. But when I met you, when I knew you were the one for me, I had to do it for you, too. I had to show you I could be the man to take care of all your needs."

She was shaking her head although she knew he couldn't see her. "I never doubted that, Ty. I never needed you to prove that to me. I just needed you to let me in."

His body tensed as her words struck a corner of his heart with painful clarity. "I did what I thought was my job. I was the husband that I thought I should be."

"You treated me like a business deal. Once it was closed, you didn't work as hard."

He could feel her shifting behind him, as if he wanted to break free of their embrace. He kept a hold of her hand as he turned to face her. "Felicia, sweetheart, you know I love you. You know I never stopped loving you."

She raised her head to look at him, and Ty's gut clenched at the sight of unshed tears in her eyes. "For once, that wasn't enough."

"I don't understand," he admitted. Ty had thought if he loved and cared for his wife, his marriage and his life would be perfect.

"I needed you to do more than love me. I needed you to trust me with things like you just told me, to pay attention to what I was feeling."

"I let you down," he said solemnly. "For that I am truly sorry. It was never my intention to ignore you. I just wanted to provide for us. Working and building the business was going to make our lives so much easier."

She looked at him sadly. "Working and building the business took away the life we could have had."

Felicia pulled away from him then, and Ty panicked. He grasped her hand tighter, pulling her into his arms. "No. It's not too late for us, Felicia. I can fix this. I *will* fix this."

"Ty—" she started to say, and he stopped her words with his lips on hers.

Enthralled, Felicia savored the sensual slide into Ty's passionate kiss and followed his lead. Acutely aware of his lips on hers, his hands going around her waist then down to cup her bottom, Felicia's mind whirled in the sensational feelings.

He mastered her mouth, pulling for the moans and sighs that forced her to plaster her body to his. Her arms twined around his neck, holding him close, never, ever wanting to let him go.

He'd read her mind, Felicia was certain because, when he broke the kiss, he whispered,

"Come back to me, Felicia. Come back to our home. I cannot live without you."

"And I no longer want to be without you." Her answer was honest. Pure and true. Tyson Braddock was and would always be the love of her life. She would not deny that, nor would she deny herself the happiness they shared together.

Felicia now had better insight into what Ty was going through and wanted desperately to help him get past his insecurities. Her mind was made up, despite what had happened in the past. She was going back to her husband, to their home and the family they would build together.

Chapter 8

It was Sunday and Felicia rose earlier than she had the day before. She wished she could enjoy her serene surroundings one more time before they were to return to the city. Instead she sat on the cool bathroom floor with her stomach churning and Ty holding a cool towel against her forehead.

Morning sickness was for the birds or anybody else who enjoyed this torture. For her, pregnancy was not supposed to be like this. Complaining was pointless. This she already knew. Still, when she'd finally been able to stand and rinse her mouth, Ty had carried her back to bed. She'd glimpsed at the clock, only to moan as she saw it read four-forty in the morning.

She must have immediately fallen back asleep, because when her eyes blurrily focused on the clock again, it was after eleven. Moving slowly, she'd gotten out of bed and walked through the cabin looking for Ty. Once again, he was nowhere to be found. Deciding that he might have gone for another walk since she had been sleeping the morning away, Felicia grabbed some clothes and headed into the bathroom to shower. They were supposed to be leaving that afternoon, so she wanted to be ready whenever Ty returned.

Ty was cutting it close. Felicia would probably be up by now and he hadn't gotten back to the cabin yet. It was only about ten minutes away now, he thought as he walked. Even the thought of Felicia questioning him could not bury the fact that he'd just landed one of the biggest investors of his career. Brentwood was going to put his funds in Ty's more-than-capable hands. He was ecstatic. He only hoped his wife would share his joy.

Shifting gears, Ty began to think more about his wife and this new life they were embarking on. She'd said she wanted a house. Well, he was taking care of that. She'd agreed to move back to the penthouse with him and he was more than thrilled about that. She'd told him she would always love him—there were no words for how that made him feel. For all intents and purposes, his life seemed to be on the right track.

Just as he walked into the cabin, his cell phone rang. Ty immediately answered it. He'd said only a few words before Felicia walked in.

"I thought this was a work-free weekend," she said tightly when he'd ended the call.

"I never said that," he replied frankly.

She sighed. "That's a likely excuse."

"Come on, Felicia. You can't expect me to quit my job. I've been doing everything you've asked of me. We've spent more time together in the last few weeks than we have in the last few years. I'm really trying, but you need to cut me some slack."

Because there was a smidgen of truth to his words and she really didn't want to argue in the last few hours of their trip, Felicia backed down. Yesterday at the creek she'd agreed to move back in with him. And last night, as they'd made love in front of the fire, she'd known without a doubt that she'd made the right decision. She refused to start this new day with the same old doubts and worries.

"Fine. What was so important that Marsha had to call you up here?"

"She was returning my call. I needed to tell her that we'd landed Brentwood and what things to get ready for me tomorrow."

Felicia smiled. "The infamous Tyson Braddock strikes again," she said. Then she crossed to him, going up on tiptoe to kiss him briefly. "I'm very proud of you and your business accomplishments. I always knew you would be successful."

He drew her to him then. "My success means nothing to me if I don't have you by my side. Do you understand that?"

She nodded, the weight of his words too much for her to speak.

Less than an hour later they were packed and in the car, on their way back to the city.

"So what's going on with the investigation into your father's death?"

"What?" Ty asked, taking his eyes off the road for a minute to look at her. "Who told you there was an investigation?"

"First of all, you should have been the one to tell me. And it was Shondra. We had lunch last week and she mentioned it. But I knew something was going on from all the whispered conversations you were having with her and Malcolm."

"There is no investigation and nothing is going on."

"Don't lie to me, Ty."

He exhaled, slamming his palm on the steering wheel. "I don't want you worrying about this. We don't even know if there's anything to worry about."

"Shondra says it might not have been an accident."

Ty cursed. "I'm going to sew that girl's mouth shut."

Shifting in her seat so that she was now facing him, Felicia quipped, "I'd like to see you try that one. Besides, I'm family, too. Why shouldn't I know what's going on?"

"Because you're pregnant and you don't need to be dealing with a lot of stress. You need to be focused on taking care of yourself and the baby."

Felicia had heard this before, from her doctor. But she had assured Dr. Franz that things were going to be better for her now that she and Ty were back together. The stress of wondering if she'd be raising her baby alone had been alleviated. So why had the cramping continued?

As she'd laid in the bed that morning, she'd felt that something might be wrong. Fear and denial made her push that out of her mind and turn back to her husband. "The baby and I are fine. I'm not a piece of china. I'm not going to break into pieces if you throw something hard at me. So tell me what's going on."

Ty hesitated for what seemed like eons. "We don't really know. It just seems like there's a lot of loose ends surrounding the accident. Like Dad made a call to this woman who works at Stewart Industries."

"Isn't that where Shondra's boyfriend works?"

"Yeah. Shondra actually met him while she was trying to gather information for us."

"An office affair. That's my girl," Felicia chimed and laughed when Ty frowned at her. "I'm sorry. Go on."

"Connor talked to the woman but didn't get a lot of answers. But he has the sense that there's something going on. And that it's somehow connected to my father. And Dad made arrangements to travel to D.C. on the day he had his accident. Gloria *always* booked his travel, but she knew nothing about this last trip. Plus with the break-in and all…"

"Wow. That does sound strange. This is too much."

"I know. That's why I didn't want to tell you."

"No. I mean, it's just too much to believe that something like this happens in real life. Schemes and plots to kill are usually only in the movies or in books. You never imagine that they'll happen to you or someone you know."

"I don't want to think that my father was murdered."

She reached out a hand and touched his knee gently. "I know you don't, baby. But you owe it to Harmon to find out what happened for sure."

"Yeah. I guess you're right."

"Shondra wants to hire a PI to look into it."

"She told you that, too?" he asked, flabbergasted. "Is there anything she left out?"

"Well, she didn't mention that my husband was being the rock supporting his siblings and his mother through this horrible time. I figured that one out all by myself."

"I'm not doing anything special."

"Come on, I saw how Harmon's death affected Malcolm. He's the oldest and he didn't know which way to go. Shondra was falling apart and you kept them both steady. You never wavered. Nobody would have ever guessed the struggle you went through."

"You were there, so my struggle wasn't as hard."

Felicia held her head down, remembering the night she spent with him after his father's funeral. The night their child was conceived.

Chapter 9

Joe Dennis had been Harmon Braddock's personal driver for years. He'd been with him before his election to office and through the years before his death. And in that time Joe had learned much more than he'd ever bargained for.

People usually forgot that drivers had ears, too, so they talked around him. Said things that were most definitely private and didn't really take a second to think what Joe might do with the information.

As much as Joe liked Harmon Braddock, he had known the man's term in office was coming to an end. Things were about to go down and Joe needed to make sure that when they did, he would still come out on top. So he'd begun to pay more attention than usual. Listening and watching, keeping names and faces in his mental safe until the time was just right.

He'd taken Harmon to more than one meeting at the home of Judge Bruce Hanlon, but this time when they'd met, he went inside. It wasn't hard to bribe one of the housekeepers; everybody had a price.

Joe had stood outside the door of Judge Hanlon's office listening to the conversation between him and Harmon. What he heard only confirmed the plan he had already put into place. The plan he'd executed with the greatest of care.

After listening to the information Joe had, Hanlon was quick to negotiate. And once Joe proved his value, Hanlon had paid up. But now, with Braddock's children getting a little itchy about the accident, Joe knew he could make so much more.

So he'd called Hanlon once again, offering Old Blue Eyes one last chance to keep his name clear.

"Half a million," Joe had said without blinking an eye.

Hanlon had thrown back his head and laughed. "You're out of your mind. I'm not giving you that type of money. Braddock is dead. Nothing you have can hurt me that much."

Joe had smiled along with the stupid old man. "I have the key."

Hanlon's face had gone pale, just as Joe expected.

"Now, when can I expect my money?"

That had been about a week ago, right after Joe had overheard another conversation between Malcolm Braddock and Gloria Kingsley. He had gone back to Harmon's office to pick up some paperwork for his personnel file, and they were there.

After hearing only a few words of Malcolm and Gloria's conversation, he knew he needed to be worried about more than the police, especially since the police, as far as anyone knew, had ruled Harmon's death an accident. Unfortunately, Harmon's offspring were just as tenacious as their father. They knew something wasn't right.

Now Joe sat in his recliner, waiting for the phone call. The one that would say, *The money is in your account.* But as of yet, it had not come.

Instead, he heard a knock at the door.

Now back in the penthouse, Felicia stepped out of the shower. She and Ty had been back from Lone Star for three days. During that time, they'd had dinner with Shondra and Connor, gone back to work and moved all her things from her apartment back to the penthouse.

So she was back in the penthouse, sleeping in the bed she and Ty had picked out at a sleek new furniture store just south of Houston years ago. Yet, once again, she was there alone. At least until almost eleven-thirty Wednesday night when she'd heard Ty's key in the door. He'd come in as quietly as he could have, moving through the darkened bedroom so as not to disturb her.

Again, Felicia tried her best not to go down this road. She'd talked to her mother earlier in the day, telling Lydia of her decision to move back in with Ty. Her mother had been pleased because, in her eyes, Felicia and Ty belonged together. Still, Lydia had been quick to warn her not to expect overnight changes. The fact that Ty was willing to try was a first step.

Felicia agreed and knew that she would take her mother's advice. She would give her husband a chance to prove to her that things would be different this time. So she'd rolled over onto her side and kept her mouth shut. When Ty was out of the shower, he climbed into bed beside her, wrapping his arm around her waist and pulling her back close to his front.

He placed featherlight kisses on her shoulder, then her neck. Content with his presence in their bed, Felicia sighed into his embrace.

When his palm moved upward lightly, cupping her breast, she moaned. How was it that he knew just how to bring her pleasure, just where to touch and what to do? No man before him had mastered this.

His erection pressed persistently into her bottom, causing her to quiver with need. Then his hand slipped down her torso and stopped over her mound. She quietly acquiesced to his silent command by opening her legs slightly. His fingers eagerly slipped inside, parting her now-damp nether lips. He brushed past her tightened rosebud, and she bit her bottom lip. Then his fingers plunged inside her opening. Her entire body trembled, convulsed, then shattered into a million pieces.

In the next instant, Ty had shifted, grasping her hips then slipping his thick sex into her center from behind.

"Ty," she whispered and swiveled her hips with his next thrust.

"I missed you so much today, sweetheart," he murmured in her ear.

Shamelessly, Felicia thrust her bottom back against him, wanting his thick shaft as deeply inside of her as it would go.

"That's right, give it to me. That's exactly what

I was missing," he chanted. His fingers dug into her hips as he anchored himself firmly in her body.

Ty's senses reeled at the feel of her velvet warmth wrapped tightly around him. He'd been thinking of her all day, thinking of being inside her this way, hearing her call his name and beg him for more.

"Ty. Please," she crooned, inching her body back even more, thrusting to meet his every stroke.

She was close, he knew, and he wanted to give her the sweet release she so desperately desired. So, without wasting another moment, he reached around her, touching a hand to that erotically puckered bud at her center and first rubbing his finger over it. Then he pressed it flat with his thumb until Felicia sucked in a breath. He pulled out until only the tip of his arousal stayed inside her, waited a beat, then sank back in.

Felicia screamed his name, bucking wilder against him. God, he loved this woman.

As she rode the wave of her release Ty slipped out of her. He pushed her gently onto her back and covered her body with his. With smooth precision, he entered her slick heat once more and began riding her until his own release tickled his spine. Before long it was his turn to clench in ecstasy, to roar her name in sweet release.

* * *

It was now Friday. Felicia had cooked them a nice dinner and now waited for Ty to come home. She'd called him at the office before she left work to make sure his evening was clear. After waiting for him last night, then growing angry and then melting in his arms when he'd touched her, Felicia figured it would save her a trip on an emotional roller coaster if she simply called to check his schedule first.

Marsha had told her his calendar was clear after a four-thirty meeting. So why, at nine-thirty in the evening, was her husband still not at home? She tried to replay her mother's words in her mind. She tried to remind herself to be patient but, dammit, he could have at least called her to say he wasn't coming right home. She didn't appreciate being the sit-at-home-and-wait wife.

That was why she'd left him the first time.

Slipping her nightgown over her head, Felicia felt the all-too-familiar cramping in her lower back. She'd called Dr. Franz that morning and had been told by his assistant that, as long as she wasn't bleeding and the cramping didn't increase pain-wise, she was most likely okay. The assistant advised her to drink more water and to get more rest until her appointment next week. At her last visit, Dr. Franz had told her not to worry, but that was getting harder by the day. Whether it was about her husband, her marriage or this pregnancy, worry seemed to be her middle name.

The sound of the front door closing snapped her out of her thoughts, and she brushed her hair back and sat on the edge of the bed. She would not fake sleep tonight. Ty was going to hear how upset she was.

Ty scrubbed his face with a hand. Brentwood was beginning to work his nerves. Every day the man had another question, another scenario he needed Ty to work through for him. And because this deal with Brentwood was the biggest of his career, Ty was busting his behind to appease the man.

But at what cost?

Felicia hadn't said anything yet, but he could tell she was thinking that he'd gone back to his old ways. But when she'd let him make love to her, he'd felt her tension subside. She was right; in that area, they'd never had any problems. Still, in the light of day, he knew that it would only be a matter of time before she would say something.

He wanted to be with Felicia, he wanted to give her everything she needed, but as he'd told her before, he still had to work. Unfortunately, his job was not the nine-to-five she wanted it to be.

Letting himself into the penthouse at almost half past ten, Ty steeled himself for her frosty reception. It was too much to hope for sex to smooth the waters, he was sure.

The house was dark and he smelled the faint scent of fried chicken. His stomach growled. He'd met Brentwood at a sushi restaurant, and because the food hadn't looked remotely appealing to him, he hadn't eaten.

So he was seated at the marble-topped island in the kitchen, his jacket and tie tossed in the living room, biting into a chicken breast he'd found in the refrigerator, when Felicia came in.

She wore a black silk robe cinched at the waist and highlighting the growing mound of her stomach. "Good evening," she said, giving him a pointed glare.

Frosty greeting indeed. Ty felt as if icicles had grown on his eyelids as her gaze held his. "Hey," he said, reaching for a napkin and wiping his mouth. As he chewed, he thought of what he would say. What could he say to make her feel better?

"I called your office when I left school. Marsha said you had no more appointments after four-thirty. So I came home and cooked for us."

With his elbows propped on the counter, he continued to watch her. Cautiously.

"My four-thirty meeting was with Brentwood."

"I thought you already signed him."

"I did."

"And you met with him already on Monday."

Ty sighed. "He's very needy right now. The amount of money he's investing is significant. He needs me to hold his hand."

"For five hours?"

"I'm sorry, sweetheart. It's just necessary right now."

"Why can't someone else do it?" she asked, leaning against the doorjamb.

"Someone like who? I'm the owner of the company. I sought him out and presented this deal."

"That's all the more reason why you can pass him on to a junior broker once you have the contracts signed. You have an entire department that needs this kind of work experience."

She clearly did not understand the importance of this deal. "It's not that easy, Felicia. Brentwood and I have a relationship. That's why I met with him at Lone Star. This case is fragile. I can't just push him off on someone else."

"It's not pushing him off, Ty. It's delegating responsibilities. What's the point in having a company full of employees if you're determined to do everything yourself?" She paused then and tilted her head, continuing to stare at him.

Ty sensed that whatever was coming out of her mouth next was not going to be good.

"You met with him up at Lone Star?" she asked in a deadly calm voice. "The weekend we went away. That wasn't just a getaway like you said, was it?"

A dozen choice expletives ran through Ty's mind at his slipup. He couldn't believe he'd just told on himself. Dragging a hand down his face, he stalled for time to think of what to say.

"Felicia," he began after a few minutes and knew that it was a pitiful attempt.

She was already shaking her head. "No. Don't try to come up with an excuse. Just tell me that you had a business meeting to go to and decided to take me along as an afterthought. Just tell me that you never had any intention of putting me and our family before business."

"Sweetheart, it's not like that."

"The hell it isn't!" she raged. "Do you think you're the first man to think he can have his cake and eat it, too? Well, you're not. However, I am a bit more hurt that you would much rather cheat on me with business deals and secret meetings rather than just going to another woman."

"What are you talking about? I'm not cheating on you. Felicia, baby, just calm down. We can talk about this." He reached for her then and watched as she pulled away from his grasp, a look of pure dislike on her face.

"No, we can't talk about this. Not anymore. I'm sick of talking, Ty, and I'm sick of being the only one trying to work on this relationship."

She'd gone from yelling to that chilly, cool tone again, and Ty didn't know how to take her from one moment to the next. "Look, it's late. Why don't we just go to bed."

She gave a sickly chuckle. "I've been in bed for a few hours by myself."

Suddenly he was no longer hungry. Ty turned back to the counter and emptied his plate in the trash. Then he walked toward her.

"I've said it once and I'll say it again. I'm sorry."

"The only thing you're sorry about is that I stayed awake to approach you. As long as I keep quiet, you keep doing what you do."

She turned to walk away from him then stopped abruptly, sucking in a breath. Ty immediately went to her, his hands going around her waist to steady her. She suddenly looked really fragile.

"Sweetheart, are you okay? Tell me what's wrong."

She kept her eyes closed for another moment then opened them slowly. "I'm fine," she said tightly. "Just tired."

"You sure?" For some reason her answer wasn't ringing true.

"Yes. Excuse me, I'm going to bed now."

She moved around him and proceeded into the bedroom, and Ty let her go. But she didn't look fine. She looked as if she were in pain. The problem was that Ty couldn't decipher if that pain was physical or emotional.

To appease himself, he decided he would find out when her next doctor's appointment was. He had a few questions about this pregnancy and his wife's overall health.

And if the pain he'd seen so clearly etched across her face was on the emotional side, Ty had no idea what he would do. Getting Felicia back hadn't been easy, but there had been no question that he would succeed. Losing her again, however, was not an option.

Chapter 10

Felicia sat at the Zebrano veneer dining table on the enclosed deck at the Braddock estate with her mother-in-law. It was Saturday, and Ty was supposed to have met her here for lunch. That was over an hour ago.

So now she was finished eating—well, picking at her chicken salad—and was more than ready to leave. In the wee hours of the morning, she'd come to a conclusion—Tyson Braddock would rather be successful in business then be married to her. Felicia didn't consider herself a demanding woman. She wanted only what most women her age did: a loving and attentive husband, a house and kids. She hadn't asked Ty for anything out of the ordinary. She simply wanted her husband to be a willing participant in their marriage, in this pregnancy.

Ty, apparently, was not up for that challenge. His hours were longer, his calls less frequent, his appearances almost nonexistent. Sure, he'd courted her for almost a month, just like she'd told him she wanted. Maybe she should have specified that the courting had to last the duration of the marriage. Maybe she should have given him a detailed report of what she expected from her husband on a daily basis.

The Brentwood deal was important to him, important to his company. And she respected that. But she didn't have to accept it. There was no reason for Ty to be taking all the meetings with Brentwood and enduring all the man's insecurities. He paid people to do just that.

The fact that he chose to deal with this client and this account totally on his own was, in essence, his choice of his job over her. Again.

Since they'd argued at the penthouse and she'd almost passed out from the sharp pain in her stomach, she and Ty hadn't spoken about business. School was closed today, so she had agreed to the lunch at his mother's. Ty had it on his schedule;

Felicia knew this because she'd seen it on the calendar he kept on the computer at home, and she knew that Evelyn would have called the office to confirm. And yet, he wasn't here.

There was no doubt in her mind that his absence had something do with work.

Felicia's head hurt as she questioned herself. Was she being unreasonable? Was she simply overly emotional because of the pregnancy? Or was Ty really choosing business over her? And, how long was she supposed to endure this treatment? Would he be like this with their child?

This back-and-forth, on-and-off was just too much for her right now. She simply didn't have the energy to be angry or hurt any longer. What she knew without a doubt was that she needed more than Ty was willing to give. And if he couldn't give it then she would simply do without—on a more permanent basis.

"When you're ready to talk, I'm here to listen," Evelyn Braddock said, interrupting her thoughts.

Her calm, attentive voice had Felicia looking up into Evelyn's dark brown eyes, which were so like her son's. Evelyn was a beautiful woman with flawless honey-brown skin. Her hair seemed to be a shade darker than ebony, softly curled and resting gently on her shoulders. She wore an expensive yet tasteful pantsuit in a buttery yellow color that accentuated her soft features.

And she was onto Felicia.

For the last hour Felicia had tried to keep up general conversation. She hadn't seen Evelyn since the funeral, which was itself out of the ordinary. When she and Ty had first been married, she'd visited her in-laws at least once a week, usually for the family dinners they had on Sundays. But over the years those dinners had dwindled. Still, she'd continued to visit and call. She and Evelyn had a good relationship up until she left Ty. She had in a sense left the entire Braddock family because there was no way she could be around them and not see or think about Ty. She had no idea how she was going to do it this time, especially with a baby connecting them.

"I'm sorry, Evelyn. I was just daydreaming."

Nodding and touching a finger to her chin, Evelyn only stared at Felicia. "You haven't called me Evelyn in years. In fact, I don't think you've ever called me by my name."

Damn. Just as she suspected, Evelyn knew something was up. "My mind is someplace else, *Mom.*"

Evelyn laughed. The full, rich sound was a surprise to Felicia. In the time she'd been there today, Evelyn had barely smiled. Instead, she'd looked pensive and worried. Felicia had simply chalked that up to continued grief.

"And you must think that my brain is someplace else also. Now I've known you since you were a teenager and you and Ty were in college. I've watched you grow into a lovely young woman. You're a gifted teacher and a good wife to my son. What you are not is a liar, so please don't insult my intelligence again."

She said it in that cool, serious manner Evelyn had about her. She spoke that way when she meant business. Funny, how her eyes remained subtle and her lips spread in a natural smile as she did so.

Felicia took a deep breath as she thought about just how much she was going to tell her mother-in-law. The lies on everybody's part needed to stop now.

"I'm worried," she started to say, then stopped because she wasn't sure how to say the rest.

"You're worried about my son."

It was a statement and not a question. Felicia's stomach clenched and she decided all this drama really wasn't worth the discomfort.

"Ty and I are separated, Mom. I mean, we *were* separated. Earlier this year I left him and got my own apartment. I couldn't stay away when I heard about Dad's death. But Ty and I still didn't reconcile."

Evelyn only nodded. "And now?"

Her hands were shaking, so Felicia propped her elbows up on the table and dropped her head. "A few weeks ago we ran into each other and we decided to give our marriage another try." She lifted her head then and looked Evelyn directly in the eye. "It's not working."

"I see." Evelyn let her hands fall into her lap. "So what now? Divorce? Counseling? What's your next move?"

Felicia didn't know whose side Evelyn was on. Her head was throbbing and she was steadily growing nauseous. She didn't want to be sitting here talking about this. She wanted to go home, to crawl into her bed and let this sickness pass her by. But Evelyn expected an answer. "The reason that Ty and I decided to reconcile a few weeks ago was because he found out that we were going to have a baby."

Evelyn's eyes brightened. "A baby?" she whispered, her hands immediately coming up to take hold of Felicia's. "You're having a baby?"

Felicia couldn't hide a shaky smile. "Yes, ma'am. I'm almost four months pregnant."

"I'm going to be a grandmother." Evelyn's eyes watered.

"But Ty and I cannot stay together," Felicia said hurriedly before Evelyn got swept away by the baby news.

"Tell me what's the problem between you two. I know it's not another man because I can see clearly how much you still love him. And I know I taught him better than to cheat on his wife."

Felicia shook her head. "No. It's not another man or another woman. I wish it were that simple."

Taking her hand from Evelyn's, she picked up her glass and sipped the iced tea slowly. "Ty is only focused on work. That's all he does, all the time. In the beginning I thought it was okay, because we were newly married and he wanted to make our lifestyle as comfortable as possible. I told him it didn't matter to me as long as we were together but you know how stubborn he is."

Evelyn chuckled. "Just like his daddy."

There was a wistfulness to that statement that Felicia couldn't miss. "After a while it just became too much. He was rarely at home and when he was, he was distant and distracted. I planned vacations and he cancelled them. I fixed dinner and he came home at midnight. I tried to talk to him and he yelled that he was doing this for us. I got fed up and I left. Then I saw him again and...and I got pregnant. I wanted it to work between us. I really did, and I thought that Ty did, too. He said he was going to work on it. But we're right back where we started. I just can't do this anymore, Mom."

"Okay, calm down. No need getting yourself and my grandbaby all upset," Evelyn said, standing from her chair. "Come with me. You need some air."

Felicia stood and followed Evelyn out onto the veranda. It was chilly outside, but the sun was high in the sky, giving off minimal heat in its wake.

"Just take a few deep breaths. We won't stay out here long. But you've lost all your color and you look like you're about to fall onto the floor." Evelyn wrapped an arm around Felicia's shoulders, rubbing them up and down, and encouraged her to take deep breaths.

Felicia inhaled and exhaled until her pulse was steady and her queasiness subsided just a little. "I don't want half a marriage."

"And you shouldn't have to settle for one. I don't know what's wrong with that boy. No, that's not right. I know exactly what's wrong with him. He's just like his daddy."

Felicia grinned. "You said that already."

"I mean this in a bad way. When Harmon and I were first married, his one goal was to prove to me that he could take care of me just as good as my father had. Since my family came from oil money, Harmon felt he had to compete. He had to work his fingers to the bone to keep me living in that lifestyle. I didn't care one way or the other as long as we were together. But he insisted. Harmon always had to be good at business. He always had to prove that he was the provider for his family. Tyson is just like him in that regard.

"All his life, Tyson has been fighting to prove himself, either to his father or to his older brother, or even to himself. He's been running this race for so long I don't think he even knows how to stop."

Felicia opened her mouth to speak but Evelyn silenced her with a look.

"But he has to stop. He's a good man but not because he can make a million dollars in a year. Not because he can schmooze billionaires into investing their money with him. He's a good man because he loves his wife and he wants to do right by her. That's what he needs to focus on. Not business." Evelyn's voice rattled with indignation.

"I don't know how to make him see that."

"It's not your job to keep showing him. He needs to come to his senses on his own. Or by me knocking him upside his head," she said, tossing Felicia a playful look. "Whichever one comes first."

Felicia laughed. "Thank you for understanding."

"Of course I understand. I told you I lived this same dilemma."

"How did you survive it? How did you stay with him?"

"I got pregnant with Malcolm. And that one act slowed Harmon down until all he could do was eat, sleep and dream about that baby. Then Tyson came and Harmon couldn't have been happier, more content. Shondra was the icing on the cake. And, Lord, did he love his baby girl."

It was Felicia's turn to comfort now. She put a hand on Evelyn's. "I know you miss him. I miss him, too. This has been really hard on you, and yet you can stand here and help me through this troubling time. You're an amazing woman."

"No. I'm just human. We have our ups and our downs but we've got to keep living." Evelyn kissed Felicia on the forehead then touched a hand to the slight bump of her stomach. "Now I want you to go home and get some rest. Your number-one priority is to take care of my grandbaby. You do whatever you need to do to keep yourself calm and healthy, and let Tyson get himself together on his own. You can't fix him, do you understand me? You can't fix this marriage by yourself."

Felicia nodded. "I understand." And she did. It was now Ty's turn to figure out what he wanted. She wasn't giving him an ultimatum. She was making a choice. For herself and for her child.

* * *

Evelyn Braddock did not condone foolishness in her children. She and Harmon prided themselves on raising mature, conscientious and intelligent children. Her husband would be angry beyond words to see what his son was doing to his marriage. Especially since Harmon had come to terms with his own faults.

Just thinking about Harmon had Evelyn's heart breaking. She'd loved him for what seemed like forever. The thought of living the rest of her life without him was at most times too much to bear.

However, she did have to bear it. She had to press on and live the life she was meant to. That was the burden for those still in the land of the living. Evelyn knew without a doubt that, as everyone lived, there would come a time when everyone would die. So she wasn't hopelessly wallowing in her grief. Still, grief lived within the chambers of her heart that were once occupied by a man named Harmon Braddock.

As such she knew that she owed it to her husband's legacy to get their son in line. Tyson was about to mess up with a good woman. A woman who was carrying her grandbaby. And she was not about to sit back and let that happen.

Meddling in her children's affairs was not one

of Evelyn's hobbies, but when they needed to be reprimanded or have some sense slapped into them, she didn't have a problem acquiescing.

Tyson and Malcolm had just arrived at the house. Tyson had missed lunch with her and his wife more than three hours ago. Evelyn wondered if he'd even called Felicia to apologize. Not that she blamed Felicia if she didn't accept the apology.

Evelyn walked down the hall toward the living room, where she knew her sons sat talking, and stopped short as their voices carried to her ears.

"Connor talked to Daiyu Longwei, but she didn't shed much light on the phone call Dad made to her just before the accident," Malcolm was saying.

"So she denied that Dad was calling her?" Tyson asked.

At the sound of the name Evelyn had not heard for years, she stood just outside of the living room and listened.

"She couldn't deny the cell phone records. She just didn't give Connor any reason why Dad would have called her. She did ask him if her job were in jeopardy."

"And what did he tell her?"

"He can't fire her for not answering his questions, Ty."

"True. But if she's involved in a murder plot…"

Evelyn kept a tight reign on her temper. Hadn't she told them she didn't want them playing investigator anymore? Granted, she hadn't acted on any of their suspicions personally, because the thought that someone could have murdered Harmon was just too much for her to bear.

From what she was hearing, however, her children were still piecing things together.

"Have we officially moved from an accident to a murder?"

Tyson waited a moment to answer. "We can't ignore the facts we've uncovered."

"And we can't put them together to make any sense out of them."

Both men were quiet.

"Okay." Tyson spoke up again. "I think it's time we decided where we go from here. Call Shawnie and let's meet tomorrow. If it wasn't an accident, we need to know sooner rather than later. And if it was, then we all need to let this go so we can move on with our lives."

Evelyn's heart raced. She'd thought they'd passed this point. It had been thirty years since she first heard that name and she'd thought it was over. Her sons' words had just proven her wrong.

Chapter 11

Daiyu Longwei had a lot on her mind.

Her computer chimed with a new e-mail but she ignored it. On the corner of her desk, the phone chirped. The receptionist was calling her. She did not answer.

Instead she folded her hands in her lap and stared out the window. Something was about to happen. She could feel it. This secret that she had guarded for the last thirty-three years was about to be revealed. She had no idea how to deal with that fact.

There was a knock at her door, breaking her thoughts, and she shifted in her chair only seconds before the door opened. Not in a million years would Daiyu have been able to prepare herself for who walked in. Yet a small part of her was not even surprised. Not in the least.

The receptionist told Evelyn that Ms. Longwei was not answering her call. Evelyn didn't care. She'd come all the way across town to meet this woman face-to-face, again, and she wasn't about to go home empty-handed. So she'd breezed past the receptionist, daring the petite blonde to get out of her chair and stop her.

As a courtesy, she did knock on the door first. However, she had no intention of waiting to be invited in. Two days ago she'd overheard her sons talking about this woman and a call Harmon had apparently made to her before his accident. Well, the "accident" that her children believed could have been murder.

It had taken her two hours to accept that notion. Harmon had come a long way since they'd first met, and he'd made plenty of enemies in his work at the DA's office. She had to assume that the list of enemies grew when he'd become a congressman. Still, she didn't want to think of one of those enemies killing her husband.

After another wave of unbearable grief, she'd

pulled herself together enough to get dressed and drive herself to Stewart Industries. She wanted some answers.

The woman behind the desk stood, and Evelyn sucked in a breath. She closed the door behind her with slow movements and without taking her eyes off the Asian beauty. It had been a long time since Evelyn had seen her, but she still looked the same. Long, dark hair hanging past her shoulders, seductively slanted eyes over high cheekbones and a round face. She looked impeccable in her conservative dark business suit.

"Good afternoon, Ms. Longwei," Evelyn said as she moved to one of the chairs across from the desk. "I'm sure you weren't expecting to see me."

To her credit, when she spoke, Ms. Longwei's voice hid the tremors Evelyn saw in her hands.

"No. I did not expect you." She nodded to the chair behind Evelyn as she resumed her seat.

Evelyn sat, keeping her gaze level. "I'm not going to waste time with pleasantries neither of us feel. I'm here to ask some questions."

"Oh?" Ms. Longwei said, lifting one elegantly arched brow.

"My husband called you the day he died. Why?"

"I did not speak with Harmon that day."

The sound of her husband's name on that woman's lips stung, but Evelyn was careful not to let it show. "But he called you. That is an undisputable fact. That tells me that he must have been in touch with you before then. Is that true?"

"Rehashing the past isn't going to benefit the future."

"And lying to me isn't going to make me go away."

"Harmon and I had spoken before then."

"Why? He told you it was over thirty years ago. I was there, remember?"

"What Harmon and I discussed is really none of your business."

In a rare loss of control, Evelyn stood and slammed her palm down on the desk. "Whatever concerned my husband *is* my business. Now, if you know something about his death, it would serve you well to tell me now before things go too far."

She barely blinked at Evelyn's outburst, but Evelyn saw the moment of sadness flash into her eyes.

"This isn't helping either of us. Harmon is gone now. We must move on."

"Move on? My husband may have been killed, Ms. Longwei. Do you expect me to move on without resolving that?"

"I can't help you."

Evelyn had already straightened feeling her serene demeanor slip back into place. "You *won't* help me," Evelyn conceded. "At one point I felt sorry for you because I thought you really loved Harmon. It was such a pity that he didn't love you the same way. Now, I don't think your feelings for him were ever that sincere. Because if you truly loved him you would want to know what happened to him. You wouldn't be able to sit here so calmly and refuse to give any information that might shed some light on this matter. That's fine. After all, he was *my* husband."

Evelyn left the office as dignified as she'd walked in, although her insides were quivering, her mind roaring with the fact that her husband had never stopped communicating with the woman he'd once had an affair with.

"Dammit!" Ty roared. He had just walked through every room of the condo and noticed that all her stuff was once again gone.

The last few days had been rough for him, and he'd known they weren't much easier on Felicia. But he was trying, he really was. Once he had Brentwood situated he would be able to focus solely on Felicia and the baby.

He just needed her to bear with him a little while longer.

Obviously, she hadn't been able to do that. For a split second he was angry with her for being so childish and walking out again. How many times was she going to run away from their issues? He couldn't keep chasing her and bringing her back. If she didn't want to be here, then he couldn't make her stay.

But damn, he wanted his wife back.

Ty dropped down onto the couch and rested his head in his hands. It shouldn't be this hard. Men had families and ran businesses every day. His father had done it quite successfully. So why couldn't he?

Without another thought, he picked up the phone and dialed Felicia's cell. When she didn't answer, he left her a message to call him immediately. A few minutes later, he realized he'd used the wrong words. So he called her back and simply said, "I love you."

But was his love enough? Clearly not. Felicia had to know how he felt about her, just like she had to know how important his work was to him. And still she was gone.

The next morning, the minute Ty got to work, he called Felicia's cell, only to receive her voice mail again. Then he did something he rarely ever did. He called the school and left a message with the secretary for her to call him as soon as possible.

He sat and waited in his office all day, not taking any calls unless they were from her. Three times Marsha had come into his office to inquire if everything was all right. He remembered grumbling something at her and waiting for her to once again leave him alone.

Finally it was after five and he was sitting in his chair staring out his office window. From there he could see the building where his penthouse was. He should get up and go home, except the penthouse wasn't really a home anymore. Without Felicia, it was simply four walls and a roof.

He'd spent the day in a whirlpool of self-pity and wondered if he'd be able to snap out of it this time.

"So this is what it looks like?"

Ty turned in his chair the moment he heard the familiar voice. Malcolm and Shondra walked into his office.

"This is what *what* looks like?" he asked, nowhere near in the mood for a sibling powwow.

Malcolm took a seat across from Ty's desk. "A man who drove his wife away for a—what's this—a third time?"

"Shut up!" Ty growled, glancing with irritation in Shondra's direction.

"Oh, don't clam up on my account," Shondra said, coming to sit on the corner of Ty's desk. "Felicia told me all about it when we had lunch a few weeks ago. And when I called her yesterday, she broke down again. You know, if you weren't my brother, I'd smack you."

"Where is she? How's she doing?" Ty implored, ignoring everything else his sister had said.

"She's a mess. Sort of like you. I can't believe that you could graduate at the top of your class and still be this stupid."

Malcolm held up a hand. "Come on, Shawnie. We said we were going to come over and try to talk some sense into him. Not berate him."

Shondra crossed her legs and glared at Ty. "But that's what he needs. He needs to be brought down a peg or two so he can stop thinking this world revolves around him and what he wants."

"I need my wife," Ty said pointedly.

"Then you should have done what you needed to do to keep her," Shondra snapped.

Ty leaped from his chair to pace along the other side of his office. "What are you two really doing here?"

"You missed lunch. Remember you suggested

I set up a time for us to meet to discuss the accident?" Malcolm went to stand in front of Ty. He put his hands on Ty's shoulders and glared at him. "You know what you need to do to get your wife back. We talked about this before. Why can't you slow down enough to enjoy your success?"

"That's easy for you to say," Ty grumbled.

"What's that supposed to mean?"

"Success has always come so easy to you. You're the oldest and the smartest. Hell, now you're even walking in Dad's footsteps directly into politics. I've had to fight tooth and nail just to prove that I'm a fraction as good as you and Dad were."

"What is this BS you're talking? Ty, you are the smartest guy I know. Like Shawnie said, you graduated top in your class even if you did go to Stanford. You can turn one million dollars into one hundred million faster than I can shower and shave. You're more levelheaded and conscientious than I could ever hope to be."

Ty shook his head. "I am not like you and Dad. I don't have those same goals. But I want to make a way for my wife and our family on my own. I don't want to live off Braddock money."

"Oh, please, you doubled your trust fund when you were just an intern at that bank," Shondra added.

"You have more money of your own than Malcolm and I combined. There's no way you could ever be accused of living off Braddock money."

"You know what I realized when Dad died, Ty?" Malcolm asked.

"What?"

"You can't take it with you. No matter how much money Dad had made in his lifetime, we didn't bury it with him. When all is said and done, all we have are the memories we make. The time we spend with our families creating lasting memories and happy moments, that's all that's important. All the rest of this stuff is superficial."

"It's materialistic and damned selfish," Shondra added. "What you have with Felicia is real and it's growing in the form of my niece or nephew that she's carrying."

Ty looked over to his sister. "She told you about the baby?"

"Yeah, she told me. You sure didn't. Ty, you should have been ecstatic to find out you were having a baby."

"I was. I mean, I am."

"Then why didn't you tell all of us immediately? Why aren't you out buying baby stuff and looking for a house and making plans? Why are you sitting in this office day in and day out trying to make another dollar to add to the millions you already have? What are you trying to prove?"

That's the question Ty had been asking himself all day long. What was he trying to prove and who was he trying to prove it to? He turned away from them, taking a deep, steadying breath before admitting, "All of this is for nothing if I don't have her in my life."

"She doesn't need all of this, bro. She just needs you," Malcolm said.

Ty was struggling for his next words when his cell phone rang. He sighed, not wanting to deal with business at this moment.

Malcolm chuckled. "Aren't you going to get that?"

"I'll get it and tell those money-hungry stuffed shirts you work with to get a life," Shondra quipped.

Malcolm tossed her a warning glare. "That's not professional."

She smiled. "No, but I'll bet it's effective."

The phone was still chirping over his siblings' comments and Ty pulled it out of the case on his hip. He looked down to an unfamiliar number on the caller ID and decided to go ahead and answer it.

"Tyson Braddock."

"Mr. Braddock, this is Nurse Brockington. I'm

calling from Houston General Hospital to let you know that your wife was just admitted."

All the air drained from Ty's lungs as the woman's words registered in his mind. In the next second, he was running from the office with Malcolm and Shondra hot on his heels.

"The contractions were coming pretty regularly, Mr. Braddock," Dr. Franz told him as they stood in the private family room of Houston General Hospital.

Ty's fingers contracted and released at his sides. All he could think about on the ride to the hospital was what would happen if Felicia lost this baby. He would be devastated, and she would most likely blame him. Hell, he blamed himself. Hadn't he been reading about the effects of stress on a pregnancy, especially in the first trimester? He should have known better. He should have been more focused on meeting her every need instead of clenching the deal with Brentwood.

No, Ty thought, as if light had just begun to dawn on his world, he should have been paying more attention to Felicia and her needs all along.

She had been telling him, over and over, what she wanted, what she needed. But he hadn't been listening. He'd been too busy building his business, making his mark. Now, if Felicia lost their child and he lost Felicia, neither the business nor his mark would mean a damned thing.

"We've put her on fluids and one dose of Ter-butaline every four hours," Dr. Franz continued.

"What's that?" Shondra asked. She and Malcolm had followed Ty out of the office, and when Ty realized he hadn't called Deuce for a ride, he told them what was going on. Malcolm had driven like a madman to get there.

"It's a medication to stop the contractions. Mrs. Braddock seems to be responding to it well. But she's not out of the woods yet."

"What do you mean? If the medication is working, then what's the problem now?" Ty asked and felt Malcolm's steadying hand on his shoulder.

"Your wife is still early in this pregnancy, Mr. Braddock. For the past month or so she's been complaining of cramping and generally not feeling well. I've been watching her carefully, and I'm afraid that if she continues on this path, she may be restricted to bed for the duration of the pregnancy. It might be the only way to save the fetus."

Ty sank into the closest chair. Shondra quickly came to his side and took his hand. "Felicia is a strong woman, Ty. She and the baby are going to be just fine."

Ty heard his sister's words along with the small measure of doubt she tried to hide.

He looked up at the doctor. "How do I fix this?"

"Part of the fix is the medication. Another part—the more important part—is that she remain stress free. That whatever has been upsetting her for these past few weeks is resolved." Dr. Franz looked from Malcolm to Ty. "Mrs. Braddock has not shared her personal life with me, but I've seen enough pregnant women to know when one is stressed out. Stress is not good for the mother or the baby. She could develop high blood pressure and that could severely injure the fetus. Or worse, she could go into preterm labor. I know that she works with children and that might be a bit on the stressful side, as well. All I'm saying to you is that she needs lots of rest and lots of calm at this point."

The doctor left the room, and Ty buried his face in his hands. "I can't lose her." He sighed. "And we can't lose this baby."

They seemed like only words but meant so much more. His heart was hammering in his chest, his temples throbbing. Each breath he took was a labor of the love he feared he might be losing. How could he have been so smart and yet so stupid? Hadn't his father always put the family first? No way would Harmon have let this happen to his wife, his future.

"You won't," Malcolm said adamantly. "Because you are going to drop everything else and take care of your wife."

Malcolm's words were spoken with such strength and convinction that Ty had to look up at his older brother, who sounded so much like his father.

"Now pull yourself together and go in that room and assure Felicia that she and your child are going to be just fine."

"He's right," Shondra added. "She needs you more than ever now, Ty."

"But she doesn't want me, Shawnie." That was the first time Ty had verbalized his greatest fear. "She left me, not once, but twice. She doesn't want me in her life, and by being so stubborn and selfish I've endangered our child. I should have just let her go."

"You don't mean that," Shondra said.

"Don't even go there, Ty. You are not a quitter," Malcolm told him sternly. "You love your wife and I'm certain that she still loves you. You're damned right to stay and fight for her."

Dropping his head, Ty heard the words of his siblings. He also heard another voice, from the man who had been his mentor and biggest supporter. Harmon Braddock did not tolerate quitting, and he was a stickler for a man owning up to his mistakes.

Ty admitted he'd made numerous mistakes

where Felicia was concerned. He'd taken her for granted, first and foremost. Never had Tyson Braddock thought his wife would leave him. Not just his wife, but the woman he loved with all his heart, the woman he knew was his soul mate.

Business had been his priority for so long, it came second only to breathing. Now, with Felicia lying in the hospital and their baby's life in peril, even breathing didn't come easily.

Leaning forward, Ty rested his elbows on his knees, holding his head in his hands. This was not how his life was supposed to turn out. It wasn't the future he had envisioned. Clearly, his plans had been completely wrong, and it was past time to right them.

Ty had spent the bulk of his life trying to impress his father, trying to be the man he thought his father would want him to be. But he'd been going about it all wrong. This wasn't what his father would have wanted for him. Ironically, for the first time in months, Ty was relieved that Harmon Braddock wasn't here to see the mess he'd made.

"I will make you proud. I will be what you wanted me to be, live the way you wanted me to live." Ty remembered saying those words as he'd been the last one standing at his father's graveside. He'd made Harmon a promise, and he'd be damned if he'd let him down now.

* * *

Ty walked into the room, hearing first the slow murmur of a machine to the right of the bed. Felicia looked pale and lost beneath the voluminous white blankets that covered her and the bed. He closed the door behind him, moving as quietly as he could while keeping his gaze on her closed lids.

His eyes stung with unshed tears as the full weight of what was going on in his life hit him. Four months ago he'd lost his father, and six months before that he'd almost lost his wife. Through it all he'd continued to work, as if that were his only saving grace. But TJB Investments hadn't saved a damn thing.

He was still grieving for his father and still messing things up with his wife. It was time to put an end to this cycle, to bring some kind of balance back into his life. And it started now.

He took Felicia's hand in his, rubbing his fingers over hers, and stopped when he realized she wasn't wearing her wedding ring. His chest clenched as the weight of that hit him. She'd given up on their marriage. Given up on him.

"I told them not to disturb you," she whispered weakly.

Ty swallowed before speaking, looking at her, seeing how tired she now appeared. "Informing me that my wife is in the hospital is not disturbing me."

"I knew you were at work."

"It doesn't matter where I was. If you or our child are in danger, I want to know."

She pulled her hand away from his. "The doctor says it's better now. I just have to take this medication for another day or so."

"Why didn't you tell me you were in pain?"

"When was I supposed to tell you? When you came home and slipped into bed while I was asleep?"

She didn't try to hide the heat of her words, nor their semblance of truth. Ty didn't blame her.

"You didn't want to tell me."

Taking a deep breath, she looked away from him. "I just wanted it to go away. I want this baby so much, Ty. The thought of something happening to this child is just too much. I don't know what I'll do if—"

"Shhhh," he said, putting a finger to her lips. "Don't think like that. You won't have to do anything because you and our baby are going to be just fine."

"You don't know that," she said, turning her head again.

"I know that I'm going to do everything in my power to make it so."

"And now you think that's enough?"

There was so much he could have said to her.

They could have talked about this, rehashed their situation and blamed each other for the next three to four hours, but that would only make things worse. And Ty was not about to do that. "What I think is that we both need to focus on our child, on what we need to do to secure its health."

"That's easy. You need to go on with your business and I'll tend to this pregnancy. We need to stay apart. Being with you is just too much for me right now."

He heard her words and knew their truth. He heard her hurt and knew her pain. For as much as he wanted to insist that she come back to the penthouse with him, that he take care of her and make things right between them, Ty recognized what he must do.

Felicia's happiness and well-being meant more to him than anything else in this world. More than Brentwood or TJB business. More than his need to have his wife in bed with him every night. And so, with great heaviness in his heart, he said, "I understand. But I still love you and I love and want this child more than you will ever know. I'll give you your space but you can't expect me to stop caring, to not want updates on you and the baby."

"No," she said as tears slipped slowly down her cheeks. "I don't expect you to do that."

Behind him, the door opened and Ty heard Felicia's mother and father coming in.

"Oh, baby. Are you all right? I was so worried all the way over here," Lydia said. "Hi, Ty. Have you spoken to the doctor?"

Ty slipped his hands into his pockets and looked over at Marshall and Lydia Turner. He'd known and respected them for years. He could only imagine what they thought of him now.

"Yes, ma'am. I've spoken to him. He says that she's stabilizing but she needs plenty of rest and to keep the stress to a minimum." As he said the last words, he looked down once again at Felicia. "On that note, I'm going to give you some time alone with your parents."

He traced a finger along the last tear that had fallen from her eyes, wiping it away. "But I will be back in the morning."

When she didn't respond, Ty moved across the room. He stopped, shook Marshall's hand and kissed Lydia on her cheek. "It was good seeing you. And don't worry, I'm going to fix this."

Chapter 12

The next morning, Ty awoke later than usual. His alarm clock had gone off, jolting him out of the bed as if the house were on fire. He'd cursed, picked it up from the nightstand and hurled it across the room.

Falling back onto his pillows, he dropped an arm over his eyes and went back to sleep. He felt more tired than he ever had in his life. As if there weren't enough hours in the day for him to rest.

In the last hour, he'd only laid in the bed thinking over the events of last night. His wife was in the hospital. His baby in danger. And it was his fault.

That had been a big pill to swallow, but Ty had never been one to hide from his mistakes. He could be held accountable and would make amends. Felicia had accused him before of taking her for granted, of ignoring her and their marriage. Now, he could see how she'd come to that conclusion.

He now remembered that she'd often asked if he wanted to start a family with her. He'd never given her a straight answer even though having a family was one of his many goals. Admittedly, he'd wanted to wait a few more years, but at this very moment he couldn't figure out the reason for that decision.

He loved Felicia. He wanted her to have his children and for them to be a complete family. Groaning, he realized he'd taken too long to tell her that.

Now she was sick, and while he wasn't a doctor, Ty knew what he needed to do to help make her better.

It was after eight in the morning when he finally climbed out of bed and stumbled into the shower. With a towel wrapped around his waist, Ty sat on the edge of his bed and picked up the phone. His first call was to the labor and delivery unit at Houston General. After speaking with the nurse and obtaining an update on Felicia's condition, he dialed his office.

"Good morning, Marsha."

"Mr. Braddock. I've been calling your cell phone all morning. Mr. Brentwood has called twice and needs to speak to you immediately. He actually wanted to set up a meeting this morning but I wasn't sure of your schedule since I heard about Mrs. Braddock being admitted to the hospital. How are she and the baby?"

"Slow down, Marsha," he said, rubbing a hand over his goatee. "First off, Felicia and the baby are stable this morning. I'm going to be heading over to the hospital within the hour. Second, call Brandon Donovan. His number is in my Rolodex. Brandon is familiar with my plans for Brentwood. Tell him I need him to meet with Brentwood today and get him settled. I'll call Brandon later to brief him since I want him to handle Brentwood from here on out."

"You're giving Brentwood's account to someone else?"

Ty heard the astonishment in his assistant's voice and couldn't blame her. In the years since he'd started the company, he'd worked on every account personally from start to finish. He had additional brokers on staff but used them solely to handle mundane tasks. That was going to change.

"I'm delegating responsibilities. Once Felicia is

settled at home, you and I are going to meet to see which brokers are better suited for which accounts. We're going to restructure TJB."

"Okay. I'll call Mr. Donovan. And I'll take care of setting up a meeting with Mr. Brentwood. Are you going to call him personally? You know how he's going to squawk about this change."

"Don't worry. I'll handle Brentwood. If he doesn't want to go along with this change then he can take his money elsewhere." Even to his own ears, the words sounded foreign. But Ty had made up his mind. Today was a new day. A new beginning for him and his family.

Ty went to see Felicia. She looked a little more rested and was eating breakfast when he arrived at the hospital. She hadn't been thrilled to see him, but she'd seemed to accept that he was there and that he was concerned.

"How did you sleep?" he asked, knowing that she liked a lot of pillows. There were two pillows behind her head but they looked flat and uncomfortable.

She shifted a bit, being careful to keep the sheet tucked under her arms as she did. "As well as can be expected."

"I can bring you some pillows if you want. And

maybe another blanket. This sheet is terribly thin and they have the air-conditioning up so high it feels like a refrigerator in here."

The corner of her mouth turned upward in a tiny smile. "The coolness keeps everything sterile."

"And has you freezing your ass off in the process," he quipped. "So I'll bring you another blanket and some pillows later today."

"Thank you. But, Ty, you really don't have to bother."

"It's not a bother, Felicia." It really wasn't, but he knew it was hard for her to believe that.

They were quiet for a few minutes. The only sounds in the room were the blood pressure machine that went off every twenty minutes or so and the fetal monitor that had a steady humming sound.

"What's that?" he asked, pointing to the fetal monitor. He knew what it was, just not exactly what it did.

Felicia turned in that direction. "It monitors my contractions and the baby's heart rate."

"Really?" he asked, circling the bed until he was standing in front of the machine, then he picked up the strip of paper that emptied out of it at a steady pace.

"The top line is the baby's heart rate and the bottom shows the contractions."

Ty watched as the tiny needle moved up and down on the paper. The baby's heart rate was patterned, not too high and not too low, but not a perfect line either. As for Felicia's contractions, it looked like small peaks and valleys coming at a measured duration.

"How do you know how far apart they are?" he asked.

Felicia shrugged. "I'm not sure."

Ty watched as the line on the bottom went up a little higher. His eyes shot to Felicia's. "Are you in pain?"

She shook her head. "No. I'm pretty comfortable right now."

They both looked up as the door opened and Dr. Franz entered.

"Good morning, Mr. and Mrs. Braddock. How are you two this morning?" The older man was quite chipper, Ty noted. He also was not alone. As the doctor entered, so did a nurse, pushing in front of her a machine with lots of cords. Ty's heart beat quickly. What was going on?

"We're doing just fine this morning, Doctor. What's with the machine?" Ty asked defensively.

"We're going to perform a sonogram. I want to take the baby's measurements and make sure there's enough fluid around it. I've been watching the fetal strip and the contractions have all but stopped."

"But I just saw something," Ty interrupted.

"Yeah, I saw that, too. I figured Mrs. Braddock had moved or coughed or something like that to alter the monitor. The interruption is not consistent with a contraction."

Ty nodded, thankful that Felicia appeared to be getting better.

"I want to keep her on bed rest for another day or so and then maybe we'll let her go home. But only if she promises to rest as much as possible."

"She will," Ty said immediately.

Felicia gave him a scathing look. "Yes. I will rest, Doctor. But can I go back to work?"

Dr. Franz shook his head. He'd put on his wire-framed glasses and was now staring at the fetal strips that Ty had just looked at. "Ah, probably not for another week or so. I don't want you overdoing it too soon."

Ty didn't want her to return to work. He wanted her home, taking care of herself and their child. But he knew better than to say that. The look she'd given him for answering for her a few seconds ago had warned him enough.

"Do you think I should just take the rest of the school year off?" she asked.

Ty was surprised but still did not speak.

"I'll let you know after the sonogram. Trudy, are we ready?"

The nurse with the long blond ponytail hanging down her back nodded and moved to pull down the sheets Felicia had tucked so securely beneath her arms. "We're ready," she said.

"Now, Mrs. Braddock, I'm just going to remove the belts for the fetal monitor for the time being. I'll put them back on after we're finished."

Felicia nodded. Her hair was pushed back from her forehead and she looked a little pale. She was probably nervous. Yeah, she had just begun to gnaw on her bottom lip. Ty moved a little closer to the bed. To Felicia.

"Now," Trudy was saying as she lifted a tube from a rack on the side of the machine. "This is going to be a little cool." She squirted.

Felicia jumped. "A little cool is a gross understatement," she said and shivered.

Ty couldn't hold back any longer. He reached for her hand, taking it soundly in his. To his extreme pleasure, Felicia did not try to pull away.

Once the gooey substance was smeared over Felicia's stomach, Trudy handed Dr. Franz a probe. Dr. Franz immediately touched it to Felicia's stomach and looked at the monitor on top of the machine.

Ty looked down at Felicia. She quickly looked away from him to the monitor. Following suit, Ty also looked at the monitor but had no clue what he was seeing.

The screen was black with a cone-shaped center in a grainy shade of gray. In the middle of the gray was another black area. But this area had some shaky-looking movements. Dr. Franz began to speak in measurements while Trudy clicked on the small keyboard beneath the monitor.

Felicia's fingers trembled and Ty instinctively brought them to his lips, kissing each one until she stilled. Momentarily he pulled his gaze from the screen to look at her. She looked at him almost shyly and he continued to rub her hand with his.

"Here's the head," Ty heard Dr. Franz say. He immediately looked back at the screen.

"Where?" he asked.

"Here," Dr. Franz said, and pointed to the screen with his free hand.

"Well, I'll be damned," Ty whispered as he made out the almost oblong shape. That was his child's head. Amazing, he thought.

"And look, here's a hand."

Felicia gasped. "It is! It is! Ty, look at the hand."

Ty couldn't hide a smile. "I see it, sweetheart."

"Here are the heart and the kidneys. Everything looks really good," Dr. Franz continued.

But Ty wasn't really focusing on what the doctor was saying. His eyes were glued to that screen, watching this tiny life that he'd helped to create. Now his fingers were the ones trembling until Felicia reached over, touching her hand to the top of his.

"Turn the machine up," Dr. Franz told Trudy. "Let's have a listen to the heart rate."

In the next instant, the room filled with a sound that was fast and rhythmic, almost like a locomotive engine. Ty was instantly concerned. "It's too fast," he said.

Dr. Franz chuckled. "No, Mr. Braddock. It's actually perfect."

And as Ty continued to listen, to hear the heartbeat that outran his, yet matched when he thought of his and Felicia's together, tears formed in his eyes.

He was going to be a father. On the screen was a picture of his child. Inside the woman that he loved so much, was a baby, growing and waiting. Waiting on him to be the man he needed to be.

Felicia cried as she watched the screen and Ty leaned forward, kissing away the first tear as it trickled down her cheek. She leaned into him and he felt the tears he'd held at bay slipping past his lids.

A short while later, Ty left Felicia's room with even more hope that things would be better between them. He was just stepping off the elevator into the front lobby of the visitor entrance when his cell phone began to ring.

"Tyson Braddock," he answered.

"Ty, it's Gloria. I'm on my way over to Malcolm's. You need to meet us there."

"What's happened?"

There was a pause, then a sigh. "Joe Dennis was found dead an hour ago."

"They don't know how he died yet. Del's going to call me later with more info," Ty relayed.

Detective Delroy London worked out on a weekly basis at the same gym as Ty. They'd built a general sort of friendship, but when Harmon died Del had made a point of assuring Ty that the HPD was doing all that they could to wrap up the accident. Ty called him immediately after hanging up with Gloria as he drove to Malcolm's house. While Del wasn't on the case, he could still get info. He promised to keep Ty updated. It was likely that the detective had questions about Harmon's death, as well. Now with the death of the last person to see Harmon alive, those questions would undoubtedly increase.

Now, sitting in Malcolm's living room, he gave everyone the most updated information. Shondra was sitting in a deep, cushioned chocolate-brown chair with Connor right beside her. While Malcolm paced the floor, Gloria fixed them all cups of coffee.

Ty sat back on the couch, thinking that it wasn't even noon but already he'd heard the sound of his child's heartbeat and gotten the details of a man's death.

"This has to be connected," Shondra said.

Connor nodded. "I don't think there's any doubt about that. It's *too* coincidental."

"The question is, what did Joe Dennis know that may have gotten him killed?" Gloria said.

"No." Malcolm stopped pacing to face them all. "The question is who may have killed him? Because I bet that whoever did this to Joe Dennis also staged Dad's accident."

"You're probably right," Shondra remarked solemnly. Connor must have heard the despair in her tone because he took her hand in his. A gesture of comfort that Ty wished he had at the moment.

"It's pretty obvious that Joe was somehow involved. We need to find out just what he knew. And if he's dead now it's going to be pretty damn hard to do that," Ty added.

"We need to enlist some help," Gloria suggested.

"Drey St. John," was Shondra's immediate reply.

Malcolm nodded. "I think that's the logical next step."

Ty was silent, but he realized with a start that everyone was staring at him. They were all in this together. No decisions would be made without total agreement. He wanted to find out the truth about his father's death, but a part of him hated that it hadn't been an accident. The thought that someone would kill his father was too unsettling.

"Call him, hire him and let's get this done. There's a killer out there and he needs to be stopped," he said with finality.

Malcolm looked at Gloria, who was already reaching for her cell phone and punching in numbers.

Drey St. John was a strikingly exotic and devilishly handsome man. No matter how many times Gloria saw him that fact never escaped her.

It had been an hour since she'd called him. Ty had returned to his penthouse, claiming he'd had things to get done before Felicia was released from the hospital. Gloria hoped he'd gotten his act together. From what Gloria knew of her, she thought Felicia was a very nice woman. And Ty was just being a man, a selfish and pigheaded man. But Malcolm was certain his brother would come around. She'd have to trust him on that.

Shondra and Connor had left for a lunch date with Connor's father. Gloria and Malcolm had stayed at his place and waited for Drey.

Malcolm was fixing Drey a drink while she brought the folder that held all the clues they'd collected to the table and took a seat.

"It's nice to see you again, Drey," she said, falling instantly into those slanted eyes of his. The man had to have some Asian in him, although he was a shade or two darker than Malcolm.

Drey accepted the drink from Malcolm. "It's good to see you, too, Gloria. I don't think we've seen each other since the funeral."

"You haven't been to the office," Gloria quipped. She caught Malcolm's confused glare. He'd never understood what exactly his father had hired Drey St. John and his private investigation firm to do. In that regard Gloria couldn't help him out, as she didn't really know what the relationship between Harmon and Drey was, either.

"No. But I've been keeping a close eye on what happened. I figure since you called me, you and the family have some of the same suspicions that I do," Drey said, more to Malcolm than Gloria.

Malcolm took a seat. "The week after the funeral, Gloria and I were in my father's office and she received a call. The woman on the other line said that my father's death was not an accident."

"Did you get the number from the caller ID?" Drey asked, obviously interested.

"No. It came up unavailable. But when Harmon's cell phone bill came in, we found the last number he called before the accident was to a woman named Daiyu Longwei who worked at Stewart Industries," Gloria responded.

"As far as I know, my father didn't do any business with Stewart Industries," Malcolm said.

"Strange," Drey whispered.

Malcolm sighed. "It gets stranger. Shondra applied for a job at Stewart Industries. One of her intentions was to find out what my father's connection was to the company but instead she fell in love with the owner."

Drey grinned. "An unexpected development."

"That it was. But it worked out to our benefit. When Connor Stewart found out the real reason Shondra was at his company, he was initially pissed, but then he wanted to help us find out what really happened. Dad's last call was made to the direct line of a woman named Daiyu Longwei. Connor spoke to this woman, but she denies ever receiving a call from Dad and says she doesn't know anything about the accident. Plus, Dad booked travel to D.C. on the very day he had his accident."

For a moment Drey remained quiet. He looked to be contemplating all that Malcolm had said.

"I know you've heard about Joe Dennis's death by now," Gloria said. "We think this is too much of a coincidence to let it slide. So we decided to hire some professional help. That's where you come in."

"You're right. There is no such thing as coincidence. There's a connection and I'll bet if we find it, we'll find the killer."

"So you think it was murder, as well?" Malcolm looked relieved.

"I think that Harmon Braddock was a very cautious man. He was an excellent driver and he was smarter than just about everyone he worked with. He wouldn't have driven his car off the road. And he wouldn't have been driving himself to the airport unless the trip he was taking was top secret."

"Anything top secret reeks of conspiracy, lies and betrayal. All reasons to commit murder."

Malcolm exhaled, rubbing his face. Gloria placed a hand on his shoulder. *So they were involved now?* Drey thought. He looked at two people he'd seen in passing for a few years now. He guessed they were probably a good couple. They certainly looked comfortable together.

"So where do we go from here? I think this Longwei woman knows something she's not telling us."

Drey had a sick suspicion that this was true.

"What are your rates?" Malcolm was asking.

Drey stood and picked up the folder that he suspected held the phone records. "Harmon was a good man. We had a great relationship. There's no way I can charge to find the person responsible for his death."

With that said, Drey left Malcolm's apartment with the promise to call him the moment he found out something.

He knew exactly where his first stop would be.

Ty had a vicious headache. He was back at the penthouse after a two-hour phone conference with Brentwood. His newest client was in no way pleased that Ty was handing him off to an associate broker in his firm. But Ty was not budging. After an hour and a half of assuring Brentwood that

Brandon Donovan would do the job well, he'd finally given Brentwood an ultimatum: he could work with Brandon or he could take his money and have someone else invest it.

A month ago—no, a week ago—Ty would not have dared say such a thing. But then a week ago his wife hadn't almost lost their child due to his neglect. That was a road he'd rather not travel again, ever.

With that said, Brentwood had immediately calmed down, asking questions about Brandon's education and track record. Brandon was one of Ty's brightest protégés; Ty would not have given him the account otherwise. He'd even agreed to have dinner one night next week with Brandon and Brentwood to assure the change went over smoothly. Brentwood wanted to have the dinner tonight, but Ty had other priorities.

He'd just come from the bathroom where he'd swallowed two aspirin when the doorbell rang. He answered it and was a little thrown when the neatly dressed man asked him his name. He gave it and accepted the envelope that the man extended to him.

Closing the door, Ty opened the envelope, praying it wasn't another work issue. He hadn't realized how difficult it was going to be to scale back on his work hours. He was heading to the kitchen to fix himself a sandwich, then he had to leave for another appointment. As he did, he scanned the papers he'd pulled out of the envelope.

He stopped cold as he read the bold print title: *Complaint for Absolute Divorce.*

Chapter 13

It was time for Daiyu to get off from work. Drey had timed his appearance perfectly. She was a stickler for professionalism, so she would take offense to him wanting to discuss outside business during business hours.

He'd taken the day going over Harmon Braddock's records, the ones that Gloria had boxed up and had couriered to his office. So far he hadn't come across anything that would suggest a conspiracy or a setup.

Admittedly, he'd only been half looking. Daiyu's

involvement was a puzzle to him, one that worried him more than he could explain.

Stepping off the elevator, he'd walked through the small waiting area of the human resources department of Stewart Industries. He smiled and waved to the receptionist as she was packing up her belongings for the day. He knocked on the door, then entered on his mother's command.

"Hello," Daiyu said with a smile. She was just closing down her computer, her purse and briefcase already on top of her desk. "This is a wonderful surprise."

"Hi, Mom." Drey went around the desk and kissed his mother's smooth cheek.

"What brings you down here? There is nothing wrong, is there?"

His mother worried about him like he was still a child. Drey hated that. He hated that there was ever a moment that his mother worried at all.

"Nothing's wrong. I just needed to talk to you about something."

"What is it?" she asked, pulling out her chair and sitting down.

Drey sat on the edge of her desk and looked at her for a long moment. She was beautiful. No matter how many times he'd stared at her, he never got over how beautiful she really was. And she was sad. She had been for most of his life. Drey attributed that to the loss of his father, Officer Ronald St. John.

"I've got this new case," he began.

"You work too hard," she chastised.

Drey smiled then glanced around her office. "I learned from you."

"Don't be funny."

"Seriously, Mom, about this new case." He cleared his throat. "Your name came up."

"What? Me? How would I enter into one of your investigations?"

"The family of Congressman Harmon Braddock have hired me to look into the accident that claimed his life." Drey purposely stopped there to gauge her reaction.

"I still do not know how I would be involved."

"He called you. On his cell phone, he called you, one hour before his car crashed. I've checked the cell phone records three times. I even had my trace guy search the line again. He dialed your direct line here at work."

Daiyu's only movement was a shifting of her hands on her lap.

"How did you know him?"

Daiyu looked away momentarily, then met his gaze. "I had information that he needed."

"What kind of information?"

"Something that the congressman was look-ing into."

"Mom, I need to know what your involvement with him was."

Her dark eyes bore into him and Drey felt a tightening in his chest. What was she about to say?

"I reported some international fraud that has been going on here. All kinds of things—smug-gling of goods, bypassing customs, duties and tariffs… Congressman Braddock was investigat-ing the matter. That is how I was involved."

"Fraud? Why didn't you go to your supervisors or the owners of the company? Why go directly to Harmon Braddock?" How did she even know to go to Harmon? he wondered. Daiyu neither worked nor lived in his district.

"Are you asking if I caused his accident? Do you think I had something to do with his death?"

She stood to her full length in front of him, her chest heaving as she was clearly upset—or afraid, he couldn't quite tell. All he knew for sure was that he felt like an ass for interrogating his own mother.

So, taking her hands, he tried to calm the situa-tion. "I am simply trying to answer some questions for my client. I'll need to know more about this fraud Harmon was looking into for you. If you have any correspondence between the two of you, any evidence, I'll need to see it."

"I could lose my job," she said evenly.

"Mom, that was a risk you took when you went to the congressman in the first place. Whatever wheels you set in motion by doing that are going to keep rolling until we find out who is behind both the fraud and Congressman Braddock's accident."

She pulled her hands away from his and walked across the office.

"Is there something else you're not telling me?"

Daiyu did not answer immediately. She stood with her back to him for endless moments. Then she turned, looked her son directly in the eye and said, "There is nothing else to tell you regarding Harmon Braddock."

Ty had been driving for hours. The sky above was so dark now he had no idea what time it actually was. He pulled the Aston Martin into the garage at the Braddock estate and sat there long after he'd turned the car off.

From the moment he'd seen those papers, his mind had been in turmoil, his heart, his hopes and dreams shattered. He'd concluded this morning that TJB Investments, his house, his cars, none of them, meant anything to him without Felicia. That fact had struck him like a vicious blow as he'd read the documents requesting their ties be severed.

How could she do this so callously? How could she simply give up without a fight? Even as he asked himself those questions, Ty realized that she had fought. Each time she'd waited up for him and asked him to take time off with her. Each time she'd begged for them to start a family. She had been fighting to save their marriage. And he had ignored her.

Self-examination was a hard task. It was even harder when all the negative strikes accumulated rested with him.

Losing his wife and his family had never been a concern to him. Now it just wasn't an option.

He stepped out of the car and walked into the house. And was surprised to see his mother sitting in the kitchen with a cup of coffee in one hand, another cup sitting across from her.

He went over and kissed Evelyn on her cheek. "Hi. What are you doing up?" he asked.

"Sit down," she said simply in a clipped voice.

Ty raised a brow and sat down when she returned the favor. "What's going on?"

"I was about to ask you the same thing. But that would be a waste of time since I already know."

"Mom, it's late and I just want to call the hospital and check on Felicia then go to bed."

"You're staying here tonight?"

"Yeah, I'm too tired to make the trip back into town." The truth was he was too hurt to go back into that penthouse without his wife. To face the divorce papers he'd thrown on the floor as he marched out.

"That's fine because you and I need to talk."

"I'm really tired, Mom," he heard himself complain.

"I'm really tired, too, Tyson. I'm tired of watching you destroy something good. Now I'm going to brush off the fact that you didn't tell me that I was going to be a grandmother personally."

"I was going to tell you," he interrupted.

"When? When Felicia gave birth?" Evelyn waved her hand when he began to respond. "It doesn't matter now. The more important issue is what you're doing to your marriage."

That was the last thing he wanted to talk to anybody about, especially his mother. But if he knew anything about Evelyn Braddock, he knew there was no stopping her when she had something on her mind.

"Felicia and I are going to be okay," he said simply.

"Why? Because you say so?"

"No. Not just because I say so." He exhaled deeply. "Because we belong together."

Evelyn nodded. "I happen to agree with that point. But I don't agree with how you're proving it."

"Mom—"

"Don't 'Mom' me. Felicia and I had lunch. You know that day I was supposed to have lunch with both of you? Well, anyway, when you neglected to show up, Felicia got upset. She told me everything that's been going on with you two."

Ty dropped his elbows on the table, letting his head fall into his hands. "I know I messed up. And I'm going to make it better."

Evelyn reached out a hand and lifted Ty's face to look at her. "How are you going to make it better?"

"I'm going to stop working so much. I even passed on my biggest client to one of my associates."

Evelyn only smiled. "And you think that's enough?"

"That's what she wants. She wants me to be with her more, to be there for her and the baby more. And I'm willing to do whatever I have to for her happiness."

"What about *your* happiness, son? What are you going to do six months down the road when you start itching to get back to work?"

"I don't understand." Ty shook his head, trying to figure out what his mother was getting at. For a moment he thought she was going to lash out at him about how he was treating Felicia. Now it seemed like she was on his side. "What do you suggest I do?"

"I suggest you think about what it is you really want out of life and why you want it. Listen, your father and I went through a similar point in our marriage. Harmon was determined to make as much money as I already had in my trust fund. He desperately needed to prove that he could support me and keep me in the manner in which I was brought up.

"But that wasn't what I needed. I loved your father for the man that he was. He didn't have to prove anything to me, or to anyone else for that matter. You see, he kept thinking that he had to be what everyone else expected of him, instead of just being himself. It took him a long time to get a handle on that."

Ty thought about her words as he sat back in his chair. "I'm not like Malcolm. I don't want to work for the cause, and the thought of politics as a career makes me nauseous. I'm not lawyer material like Dad and Shondra. So I knew growing up that whatever I chose to do I had to do it well. Better than well. I had to be the best to make up for what I wasn't."

"That's nonsense, baby. Don't you see that?

Your father and I loved you for who and what you were. Your sister and brother love and respect you for those same reasons. And Felicia, she fell in love with an underweight college student who hated to iron his own clothes." Evelyn chuckled. "Do you think that all your focus on your career is going to change the way any of us feel about you?"

He scrubbed his hands over his face. "I think that it's important for a man to know his place, to take care of his family, to be a provider."

"Tyson, you can provide for a small village of families on the money you make in three months. You're pushing yourself too hard and you are the only person that believes that type of behavior is necessary."

"I have to be a good father. Dad would be disappointed if I wasn't." Ty stared at the refrigerator to avoid the compassion and the hurt he saw in his mother's eyes. "And I have to show Felicia that I can be what she needs also."

"When I was younger and somebody would tell us what we had to do, we'd say, 'I don't *have* to do anything but stay black and die.'" She chuckled and stood, pulling her son out of the chair to embrace him in a tight hug.

"Felicia loves you like a woman should love her husband. Your family loves you. Your father loved you. And that baby is going to love you whether or not you're a billionaire or a plumber unclogging somebody's toilet. That's what's important, Tyson. And that's all you *have* to be concerned with."

She left him standing there after kissing his cheek. Ty sat back in the chair, staring at nothing but thinking about everything. His wife, his job, his child, his life. But mainly he thought about his father and how his mother's words had struck home.

Felicia said she'd fallen in love with him before TJB had ever been created. She'd wanted to marry him and to have a family before he'd become an obsessed workaholic. That meant he must have been doing something right at that time. So all these years he'd been wasting time and energy trying to outdo himself. And at what cost?

At the cost of losing the one thing that mattered most to him.

Two days later Felicia was released from the hospital and went back to her apartment. As she looked around at the stark white walls, she felt like crying. No way could she bring her baby into this house. That's what it was. Not a home at all.

But then where would be home if Ty wasn't there?

Shaking herself free of that pointless thought, she put a pitcher of iced tea on the table and stood back trying to remember if she had everything. Shondra had called that morning and wanted to stop by. Felicia said that was a great idea and offered to fix lunch. Of course Shondra argued, saying she could bring them something to eat, but Felicia was sick and tired of laying in that bed. This gave her something else to do between watching television, going to the bathroom and taking her pills every four hours.

She hadn't had any contractions in the last two days, so the doctor had released her from the hospital. But she knew the danger now. She knew that at any moment, if she didn't keep herself calm and get plenty of rest, the contractions could start again. She could go into preterm labor and her baby could die. That was not acceptable.

The doorbell rang and she went to answer it.

"Hey, there. You're looking nice and rested," Shondra said as she entered the apartment, then stopped briefly to kiss Felicia on the cheek.

"Thanks. But I know I don't look half as good as you."

Shondra Braddock was a knockout, plain and simple. Tall and fit, always dressed to impress. She was a bombshell that any man would be pleased to have on his arm. "Who are you kidding?" Shondra remarked as she moved easily into the kitchen.

Felicia had closed the door and was following her when she heard her say, "You're the one with that gorgeous pregnancy glow. Women all over the world are, as we speak, in beauty salons trying to capture that look."

"If they want to gain weight, pee all day long and struggle to keep down the smallest of meals for nine months, they can be my guest."

Shondra sat and Felicia did the same. She reached across the table and was uncovering the plate of sandwiches she'd made when Shondra asked, "Is that really how it feels?"

Felicia thought about the question for a moment. "Not really. Most of the time there's this unbeatable excitement. Then there's awe that outside of all the side effects, there's a real life growing inside of you. That can't be beat."

"Yeah, that's pretty terrific."

When they both had plates with potato salad and a sandwich, Felicia asked what had been on her mind for a while.

"So how are things with you and Connor?"

"Things are cool."

"Just cool?"

Shondra smiled. "Things are terrific. Connor is terrific."

And there it was. The glow of a woman in love.

Shondra probably had no idea that she had that special look of her own.

"That's great. I'm really happy for you. You know he came by the hospital one afternoon to see me. He seems really nice."

"He is. And he's thoughtful. You know how hard it is to find a thoughtful man?"

Felicia only nodded.

"As a matter of fact, that's part of the reason I wanted to see you."

Yeah, she knew and she'd been trying like hell to avoid it. Shondra and Felicia had a pretty good relationship. But the bottom line was that Shondra was Ty's sister. And the Braddocks were nothing if they weren't loyal to each other.

"What's going on with you and Ty?"

"Nothing. I've filed for divorce."

Shondra looked startled then picked up her glass to take a sip. "It's that serious, huh?"

"It's what has to be done."

"Are you sure?"

"Of course I'm sure or I wouldn't have done it. Ty and I have been having problems for a long time now. This wasn't a decision I made overnight."

"Was it a decision you made with your entire family in mind? I mean, what about the child you're carrying? You're a teacher, Felicia. You know the statistics of children growing up in single-parent households compared to ones who grow up in two-parent households."

"I also know the statistics of children who grow up around two unhappy parents versus the ones of children with one happy, healthy parent."

"Touché."

"Look, Shondra, I know you mean well, but believe me when I say I've given this a lot of thought. I would never have left Ty on a whim. I've never loved anyone but him."

"So why not fight for him?"

"I can't. Not when fighting for him means fighting *with* him. Or against what he wants so desperately in his life." Felicia took a sip of lemonade then stabbed at her potato salad with her fork.

"I see what you're saying. Ty is ridiculous when it comes to work. But I know that he loves you so much. This is killing him, Felicia."

"This almost killed my baby," Felicia said adamantly. She knew she was being a tad overdramatic. "I mean, it's not as easy as you might think for me, either. You don't know how badly I wanted to stay with him no matter what. But it's not fair to me and it's not fair to our child."

"He's going to want to be a father to his baby. There's no question about that."

"And I would never stand in his way."

"This is hard for all of us, Felicia. Especially on the heels of Dad's death. We all love you. You became one of us the day Ty brought you home from college. We don't want to lose you any more than he does."

That made Felicia smile. "I love you guys, too. And if there were any other way, if there were any compromise, I would have made it. I grew up an only child, so the closeness that you have with your parents and your siblings is something I've always envied. I wanted that for my children, too."

"You know what? When I would mess up something, and I did that frequently, my dad used to tell me not to worry, that it was never too late to fix a mistake."

With that said, Shondra refused to talk about her brother or her father or any other issues that would stress Felicia out for the duration of her time there. So instead, they finished their lunch and shopped online for baby things. Then Shondra had made a big deal out of walking Felicia into the bedroom, making sure she took her next pill and got into the bed before letting herself out of the apartment.

Alone in that bed, Felicia had no choice but to think about what she'd done. Her lawyer had contacted her with the news that Ty had been served.

He'd come to see her twice a day each day since she'd first been in the hospital. At none of his visits did he mention the papers. He spoke only of her well-being and of things that concerned the baby. He'd been thinking of names and had bought a few more pieces of furniture to match the ones they'd purchased on their shopping trip to the mall weeks ago. But he never asked her to come back to him. He never pled his case for reconciliation.

Why did that make her heart hurt instead of relieving some of her stress?

Chapter 14

Another day had gone by and Felicia was finally back to work. She'd regained some sort of normalcy in her life and was trying to make that a constant.

Ty had continued his daily visits, adding phone calls now that she'd returned to work, but he still hadn't mentioned the divorce. Tired of waiting for the ax to drop, so to speak, Felicia called her attorney and set up a meeting. There were things they needed to agree upon regarding their life together. As much as she wanted to make a clean break, five years weren't simply going to vanish neatly into the air.

Besides, they had the child to consider and provide for. Ty would be more than fair. He would give
their baby anything and everything. That was fine
with Felicia because she didn't want anything from
Ty for herself. She'd loved their penthouse and every
piece of furniture they put into it, but she would walk
away from that, too. It was easier that way.

"Tomorrow at noon." Ty spoke into the phone
while sitting in his office. "I'll be there."

Hanging up the phone, he sat back in his chair
and contemplated his life once again. Well, no,
not this time. He knew where he'd gone wrong and
he knew how he could make it better. But his plan
meant nothing if Felicia wasn't on board. His
mother and siblings had been a great support in
this time, telling him how wrong he was and how
much they still loved him, making him feel better
than he'd anticipated.

He'd been seeing Felicia even though they were
separated. No, she hadn't come back to the penthouse and he hadn't so much as kissed her since
the last night they'd made love. But he loved her
just as fiercely.

She was taking care of herself. Taking the medication to hold the contractions at bay every four
hours just as the doctor prescribed. She'd gone

back to work, and while he would have preferred she stay at home, he saw how being with her students completed her.

In all their time together, he'd never really noticed how vibrant and energetic she was when she was teaching. But on her first day back, worried and unsure of how things would turn out, he'd stayed at the school all day long and watched her from a distance. The school principal hadn't been too happy about that, but she'd come around after he'd used his Braddock charm.

As the day had progressed, he'd seen her reading to the students as they all sat around her on a colorful rug. The children—and he, too, if he had to be truthful—were mesmerized by her voice. Never had he heard *Mrs. Spider's Tea Party* read with such emotion, such genuine feeling. His heart had swelled with love for her and pity for his own selfish blindness.

He'd left the school feeling pangs of jealousy that his child would hear that voice and see her smiling face every night before going to sleep and every morning upon awakening. But he would not.

His cell phone had rung as he walked down the steps of the school. He'd answered it in an agitated voice but quickly calmed down at the news he received.

It was with that in mind that Ty called his office. "Call Mrs. Braddock and inform her that I will not be stopping by her place this evening. However, I will see her at the attorney's office tomorrow."

If Marsha had an opinion, she wisely kept it to herself. Ty was supremely thankful. As much as he appreciated all the advice and urgings from the people he was closest to, he wanted to handle his situation with his wife all by himself.

Felicia took the day off from work. The appointment at her attorney's office wasn't until four o'clock, but she needed some time to get herself together. Sure, she'd been the one to instigate the proceedings, and this preemptive meeting was a way that she and Ty could iron out all the issues so that the divorce itself would go smoothly. She'd decided that would be the best way to handle things because the last thing she needed to go through was a messy divorce during her pregnancy.

Although she didn't really believe that things between her and Ty would be messy. Ty was a fair man who would keep her and the baby's best interests in mind no matter what. To that end, Felicia didn't want anything from him except support for their child. She knew that there were women who would call her ten times a fool, but she didn't give a damn. What she and Ty had shared could never garner a price tag. She didn't want his money; she'd wanted his love.

And since she couldn't have that and his active participation in their marriage, she didn't want anything. She prayed that she and Ty could remain cordial, but she didn't believe that would be an issue, either. Ty still called her and came to see her. He was very concerned about her and the baby, and he never hesitated to offer his services for whatever she needed.

Except he never touched her. He didn't attempt to kiss her or to even hold her. When she'd told him she felt the baby move, he'd been ecstatic and had tentatively reached out a hand toward her stomach to feel for himself. The warmth that spread through her at his touch was overwhelming and it took everything in her not to throw her arms around him. She would probably always feel this way about Ty, but knew that the stand she was taking was one she couldn't afford to back down from.

Ty seemed to understand. Well, she took his silence as understanding. No more did he try to convince her that he would change and that they belonged together. All his reconciliation arguments had ceased.

That was what broke her heart and what had her

hiding in her apartment all day. It was one thing to know that she was leaving for all the right reasons. It was another to know that he was willing to let her go. But she hadn't given him much choice. Had she?

No, she answered herself for the billionth time as she dressed to go to the attorney's office.

This was the right thing for all of them. Ty needed to be free to live his life the way he wanted. He didn't deserve to have her nagging at him to be a better husband. Work was his life. He'd told her that. He had something to prove and he was determined to prove it to whomever he thought was interested.

However, she needed something different. Something she wasn't even going to look for in another man. Her ideas of a family now had to shift to her and her child. Her parents were being quiet on the situation all of a sudden. Her mother felt like she'd given her advice and Felicia had taken from it what she wanted to use. Her father, who loved and cherished her, could not bring himself to side with either her or Ty. He simply wanted what was best for his grandchild. And Evelyn, bless her heart, had come to see Felicia at the hospital and again when she'd come home. The woman was possibly the biggest source of strength Felicia had ever had.

Absolutely nothing got the best of her. Evelyn still believed that Ty and Felicia would work it out but told Felicia to stick to her guns. She had also told Felicia that she'd always be family.

So it was with slow but determined steps that Felicia entered the offices of Friedman, Johansen and Clark, located in one of the many skyscrapers in downtown Houston. She heard her own voice, small and just a little shaky, as she told the receptionist who she was and her reason for being there.

Ty and his attorney obviously hadn't arrived yet, since she was the only one in the waiting room. She took a seat in the burgundy chairs, forgoing the many magazines spread out on the table before her. Instead, she placed her purse in her lap and looked around the office.

The plush carpet was hunter green. The walls separated by a cherrywood chair rail, a paisley-print wallpaper on the bottom half and the top half painted burgundy. The receptionist sat behind a marble-topped, mantel-like desk; once she was sitting, Felicia could only see the top of her head. She could hear the phones ringing and wondered if every call was another couple getting divorced.

Her heart thumped and her hands shook a little, but Felicia willed herself to calm down. This had to be done. She would feel better when it was finished, but it had to be done regardless. She was in the midst of psyching herself up when she heard the receptionist calling her name.

"Mrs. Braddock?"

Felicia jumped up out of her seat. "Yes?" she answered, wondering now if she would keep her last name after the divorce.

"They're ready for you in conference room A. It's just down that hall and around the corner," the receptionist said as she stood and pointed.

Felicia smiled. "Thank you."

She walked toward the door with her fingers gripping her purse for dear life. At the door she paused and took a deep breath. Her reaction was ridiculous. She and Ty could no longer live together as man and wife. That didn't mean they couldn't be friends, that they couldn't share this child and this child's life like two mature adults.

Steeling herself for what was to come, she turned the knob and entered the conference room.

Felicia's first reaction was that she was in the wrong place at the wrong time. Her second reaction, when she searched the many faces staring at her in the room and found Ty's, was that she was going to wring his neck!

Instead, she tried to remain as calm as she could when she asked, "What have you done?"

Instead of answering, Ty simply walked over to her, reaching for her hand. When she only stared down at his, he whispered, "Please. Just go with the flow for a minute."

It wasn't because his voice sounded so sincere, so husky and so damn sexy that she almost melted into a puddle right then and there. And it wasn't because sitting around the long conference room table were both her parents, Ty's mother, Malcolm and Shondra. Well, okay, yeah, it was precisely for that reason that she went ahead and took his hand. But she did not look at any of their relatives as he led her to the empty chair at the far end of the table.

When she was seated, Ty went down on one knee.

He took her left hand in his, rubbing along the ring finger where her wedding ring should have been. Uncomfortable by the way he was gazing down at her bare hand, Felicia tried to pull away.

Ty held firm, lifting his gaze up to meet hers.

"When we first met, I told you that you were different and that's why I was so attracted to you," he said. Her entire body stilled.

He was more than handsome in his black designer suit, crisp white shirt with platinum cuff links and sharp turquoise silk tie. His caramel complexion was perfectly enhanced by the dark goatee he'd let grow in. His dark eyes bore into hers as if searching for something she wasn't sure she had to give.

"I knew at that exact moment that once I got you, I would never let you go."

"Tyson," she whispered, not willing to listen to anymore. Her resolve to end this marriage was shaky enough with him buttering her up.

"No." He shook his head adamantly. "Please, let me finish and then you can do or say whatever you want." He waited a beat for her response.

She found herself nodding her head positively, although she didn't have a clue why.

"I always thought I needed to prove myself, to my parents and the rest of my family. And then when I met you, I felt compelled to do everything right by you. I foolishly thought that working my butt off to make more money was the right thing. On some level I even thought that the more successful I became, the more you and my family would love me.

"My father used to say that sometimes the smartest man could be the dumbest ass. I'll be claiming that title today. Because where you and our marriage were concerned I royally screwed up."

Somebody sniffled. Felicia thought it was probably her mother but she did not turn to make sure. Her gaze was riveted on Ty.

"I should have been smarter. I should have listened." He was rubbing her hand and looking at her so intensely he probably knew the tears were going to fall before they actually did.

Yes, she was crying. Her heart was so full with emotion already, his words simply pushed them overboard.

"But none of that matters now, Felicia. If I could turn back time I'd erase it all and do the right thing. But we both know that won't work. So, instead, all I can do is start over."

The tears were flowing in earnest now, from her eyes and from a couple other people in the room. She could hear more sniffling and ruffling around like somebody was looking for tissues.

She tuned out everyone and everything but Ty. Obviously he was doing the same thing because he only looked away from her to reach one of his hands into his jacket pocket. When he pulled out a small black box, Felicia's breath caught and she sobbed. Shaking her head, she tried to will the tears to stop. Her vision was blurred and she knew she wanted to see what he had in that box with twenty-twenty clarity.

His hand shook a little as he opened the box. The women in the room gasped but Felicia remained quiet. She couldn't speak, could barely breathe. The diamond was huge and sparkly, and in the princess cut she favored. The surrounding bands were platinum with smaller diamonds for added enjoyment. It was gorgeous, but she couldn't open her mouth to tell him that.

"Wait, there's more," he said then set the ring box on her lap and reached into his inner pocket to pull out an envelope.

"When I did this the first time, I told you how much I loved you and how I wanted you to share my life with me. I put a ring on your finger and asked you to marry me and you said yes.

"I guess you could say we've been there and done that. So this time, not only am I presenting you with another ring but I'm giving you the deed to a house. I asked you once what you wanted and your answer was your family and a home.

"I'm not simply asking you to be mine this time, Felicia. I'm asking you to trust me with your happiness and your heart. To trust that I can be the husband you want and the father our child deserves. I'm asking you, Felicia Turner Braddock, to marry me, again."

Her heart was pounding a mighty beat. Felicia

wondered for a moment if everyone in the room could hear it.

"You're supposed to answer him, baby," Felicia heard her father whisper when she was still trying to find her words.

Somebody laughed. It sounded like Shondra.

Felicia cleared her throat. "I…um…I don't know what to say to all that," she finally managed.

"Say what you feel, sweetheart. What you feel in here." Ty tapped a hand over her heart then let it fall down to her stomach. "And here."

That was it. She knew it and so did he. "How do I know for sure it will be different this time?"

"Nothing in life is certain. My dad used to tell me that, too." Ty glanced momentarily heavenward. "Man, I miss him. And I hope what I'm doing now is pleasing him more than any business deal I've ever closed.

"But I can start by telling you that I took your advice. I passed Brentwood on to Brandon Donovan. And next week, Marsha and I are going to go through all the accounts and divide them between the appropriate junior brokers. It's really going to be different this time. I'm going to be different because there is nothing more important to me than you and our child."

"Say yes. Say yes," Shondra cheered.

Malcolm shushed her and Felicia smiled.

Everything he'd just said, everything he'd done, was all that she'd wanted from the beginning. She'd told Ty he needed to win her back and he'd done it, in spades. She should have known Tyson Braddock would never lose a challenge. "Yes. I will marry you, again."

Chapter 15

They hadn't all been together since Evelyn's birthday in August. But this Sunday all the Braddocks were joined by the Turners and their close friends, including Drey St. John, Senator Ray Cayman and Judge Bruce Hanlon at the Holy Trinity Church.

When the morning service was over, Reverend Vereen called for the organist to play the wedding march while Ty and Felicia joined hands and walked once again down the aisle.

Felicia felt as nervous, and as sure, as she had the last time they'd taken this walk. Butterflies flitted about in her stomach. No, that was her baby. The baby she and Ty would soon welcome into this world.

Shondra, Evelyn and her mother had taken her shopping for a suit that would fit when Ty suggested they renew their vows. The cream-colored Donna Karan dress and matching jacket looked sleek and classy on her ever-changing frame.

Ty wore Versace, his favorite. The chocolate-brown suit enhanced his light complexion and his muscular build. Felicia had spent half the service simply looking at him, he looked so good. If truth were told, it wasn't just that Ty looked good. It was that this felt good, it felt right.

They'd come a long way, she and Ty. Felicia believed that it was all for a reason, it was all leading to this deeper commitment they were about to make to each other.

Now they stood at the altar, Reverend Vereen looking at them with a crinkly yet knowing smile. He'd married them ten years ago, and he would probably christen their baby.

"What God has brought together, let no man put asunder," he whispered to them.

Their arms were locked and Ty reached up his free hand to touch hers, pulling them closer together.

Reverend Vereen read the scripture in his regular, solemn tone and the small ceremony began.

When the time came for the vows, Ty began with, "Felicia, you are and will forever be the love of my life."

Her heart quite simply melted in her chest at his sincerity. So caught up was she in Ty and his words that when it was her turn, she had to blink away tears and concentrate on what she had planned to say.

Her words began slowly, succinctly, as she wrapped up her new vows to her husband. "And I will love you and cherish you and honor you and your accomplishments all the days of our lives."

Neither of them heard the music as it played behind them. In their world only they existed. The kiss they shared was more than enticing, more than alluring. It was renewing and rejuvenating. It was their second chance.

The congregation clapped, smiles were broad and laughter loud. It was a joyous celebration for the Braddock family, a stark change from the ominous grief that had ushered them through these doors months before.

However, one member of the congregation still felt a heaviness on his shoulders, and immediately after congratulating the lucky couple, he made his excuses and drove off.

Drey sat in his car, a file marked "Harmon Braddock" in his hands. In that file was everything he'd found out since he'd been working on this case. Mr. Braddock's children seemed to think there was something strange about the so-called accident that had killed their father. Drey was inclined to believe them. In fact, he'd thought that ever since he heard of the accident.

He'd gone to the scenes himself to investigate, of course. And got a friend at the local police office to let him look at their file. The reports in the PD file indicated that the skid marks on the road were consistent with a car losing control and the median strip was to the left, approximately thirty to fifty feet from where the car was found. Braddock must have been traveling in the far right lane, preparing to take the exit.

Drey tapped the folder on the steering wheel. The exit he would have taken led to the airport. Gloria hadn't known about any travel plans Mr. Braddock had prior to the accident, and Gloria usually knew the man's every step. "So what was in D.C. and why were you going there?" Drey asked aloud.

He imagined Harmon Braddock dressed in one of his dark suits, riding along in his silver Mercedes. That car was usually driven by Joe Dennis, the driver whose body had been found recently in his apartment. As far as the police report went, it didn't appear to be a robbery. There was no forced entry and nothing looked out of place. So how did Joe Dennis die? Drey couldn't wait for the autopsy report to come back.

PI work was like underwater treasure hunting. There was a pool of questions and he needed to jump in, move things around, shake them up, until he found the answers.

Today there was one answer he had a feeling he didn't want to know. But Drey took his job very seriously. He always did whatever was necessary to get his clients results. That these clients were the children of his mentor meant that he would go above and beyond his normal protocol.

Even if it meant uncovering things about the woman he loved most in this world—things he was sure she would like left alone.

Mildly disgusted with himself for procrastinating, Drey tucked the file under his seat and climbed out of his car. He moved up the familiar walkway, noting that the chill of winter was on its way. His mother's garden had begun to look a little sickly. She'd be out here working on it soon, pulling up the weeds and prepping the ground for the winter chill. She did it every year without fail. And in the spring she'd come out and do it all over again.

He used his key to let himself in and closed the door quietly behind him. It was a Sunday afternoon, so she'd most likely be in the den reading. Drey walked through the house he'd grown up in, memories assaulting him with every turn. He'd had a great childhood, his mother and his father, caring and loving parents, raising him to be an honest and loyal citizen.

"Well, hello there," Daiyu said, looking up from her book as he walked into the den.

"Hi, Mom." Drey stood by her chair and leaned forward to kiss her cheek. Sunlight streamed through the bay window, casting gold rays across his mother's lap and along the floor. She'd made a few changes to the room since the last time he was here. There were still no curtains at the bay window; Daiyu didn't like curtains. She liked the light and the clean lines the windows of her Cape Cod house displayed. There used to be potted plants at the window's base, but there were now stacks of books.

Oriental rugs still covered most of the hardwood floors leading over to the fireplace and mantel. But on the mantel, where there used to be a row of statues, now stood candles in different shapes and colors. Trained to pick up little inconsistencies and changes, Drey closed his eyes. He knew he needed to stay in the investigator mode for this conversation. But this was his mother. This was her home. The personal connection was tough and made what he had to do the most difficult task in his life.

"Drey, is something wrong?" Daiyu asked, closing her book and looking up at him. "You look distracted."

Drey took a deep breath and sat down on the black leather ottoman that always sat beside the chair and served more as a table than a footrest. Daiyu put a hand on his shoulder then rubbed his head.

"You look so tired. I keep saying you work too hard."

Drey rested his elbows on his knees and replayed in his mind how he would say what needed to be said. The words sounded normal enough—in a dysfunctional family full of drama. But to his mother, they would be more than strange, more than disconcerting, invading their peaceful life.

"The other day I asked you how you knew Congressman Braddock," he said, deciding that it was well past time to get this over with.

Her hand stilled on his neck, then slid slowly down to his shoulder. "Yes."

"You told me you contacted him in reference to some sort of fraud you suspected at Stewart Industries."

Her hand fell away from him completely. "Yes."

"Thirty-three years ago you were part of an international exchange program with Stewart Industries."

"Yes. That is how I came to stay in America. My student visa would have expired after I graduated, but my internships with Stewart helped me to stay here until I gained citizenship."

"You were in Dallas at the National Business Conference."

Beside him Daiyu shifted. Her book fell onto the floor. Drey leaned forward picked it up and ran his hands over the spine. "Harmon Braddock was in Dallas attending a criminal justice seminar. You were in the same hotel."

Drey looked over at his mother. Her hands were in her lap, wringing. Her gaze stayed straight ahead, not really focusing, but avoiding.

"That's where you met him."

"It was...so long ago. I must have forgotten," Daiyu said slowly.

Drey stood and walked to the window, placing the book on the window seat. "You know what I thought I'd forgotten? After Dad died and I was walking home from school, a big shiny car pulled up beside me and came to a stop. The back passenger door opened and a man stepped out. He wore a suit and I remember thinking that's how I would always remember Dad. In the suit he wore as he lay lifelessly in the coffin.

"The man walked right up to me and he called me by my name. He knew me but I had no clue who he was." Drey turned to face her. "That was the day I met Harmon Braddock."

"Son, I do not know where you are going with this…"

"I'm going to ask you again, and I really need you to be honest with me this time, Mom. How did you know Harmon Braddock?"

Daiyu stood slowly. Her worst nightmare was becoming a reality. She'd known the other day when Drey had come to her office asking her about Harmon that her secret was now about to be revealed.

Foolishly, she'd thought that with Harmon's death she would be safe. But that was not true.

Drey had always been a curious child. And she was so proud when he announced he was going to study criminal justice in college and follow in Ronald's footsteps to become a cop. Drey had loved Ronald almost as much as she did. The death of her husband in the line of duty had been hard on them both.

Then Harmon appeared again, offering to help Drey get through it. She was instantly against the idea but knew that to deny a man like Harmon Braddock—who was a powerful district attorney by that time—would almost certainly guarantee their secret would be revealed. So she cooperated.

Drey came to adore Harmon and appreciated all that the man did for him. Daiyu swallowed the painful secret and tried to live a normal life.

But all that had changed the day of Harmon's accident.

"I met him at the conference, yes." Although Daiyu had kept this secret to protect him, she would not stand here and blatantly lie to her son. She loved him too much for that.

He let out a sigh. "Why didn't you tell me that the other day?"

"I did not want you to ask what I know you are thinking now."

She watched him slip his hands into his pockets. He was waiting, in that patient no-nonsense way of his, he was waiting for her to tell him everything.

"Your job is very important to you, son. I know that. I also know that Harmon Braddock filled the void left by Ronald's passing. I will forever be grateful to Harmon for that."

"I need to know how you're connected to Braddock and this case, Mom. I need to know now."

Daiyu could do nothing else but nod in agreement. "I am going to tell you how I knew Harmon Braddock. But first, I am going to assure you that I did not speak with him the day of the accident. He called me but I was not in my office. The next thing I knew there was the accident and he was gone."

"What did he call you for? Is the fraud at Stewart Industries true?"

"Yes, somewhat." She nodded. "I did suspect some things and Harmon agreed to look into them for me. But he probably was calling me about something else. Something that we had been discussing a lot lately. Sort of a disagreement."

"What would you and the congressman disagree about?"

Straightening her back, Daiyu looked into the eyes of the baby she'd carried for nine months and raised for thirty-three years. He was a man now and just as Harmon had tried to convince her, a man had a right to know who he was.

With Harmon's words and the memory of their time together still fresh in Daiyu's mind, she said, "Ronald St. John was not your biological father. Harmon Braddock was."

DON'T MISS
THIS SEXY NEW SERIES
FROM KIMANI ROMANCE!

THE BRADDOCKS

SECRET SON

*Power, passion and politics
are all in the family.*

HER LOVER'S LEGACY by Adrianne Byrd
August 2008

SEX AND THE SINGLE BRADDOCK
by Robyn Amos
September 2008

SECOND CHANCE, BABY by A.C. Arthur
October 2008

THE OBJECT OF HIS PROTECTION
by Brenda Jackson
November 2008

Was her luck running out?

GAMBLE ON *Love*

The second title in The Ladies of Distinction…

MICHELLE MONKOU

"Black American Princess" Denise Dixon has met
her match in sexy, cynical Jaden Bond. But as their
relationship heats up, she knows their days are numbered
before her shameful family secrets are revealed.

THE LADIES *of* DISTINCTION:

They've shared secrets, dreams and heartaches.
And when it comes to finding love, these sisters
always have each other's backs.

Available the first week of October wherever books are sold.

KIMANI
ROMANCE

She was beautiful, bitter and bent on revenge!

Tender SECRETS

ANN CHRISTOPHER

Vivica Jackson has vowed vengeance on the wealthy
Warners for causing her family's ruin—but that's before
she experiences Andrew Warner's devastating charm.
After the would-be enemies share a night of fiery passion,
each is left wanting more. But will her undercover
deception and his dark family secret lead to a not-so-
happy ending to their love story?

"An exceptional story!"
—*Romantic Times BOOKreviews*
on *Just About Sex*

Available the first week of October wherever books are sold.

KIMANI
ROMANCE™

For All We Know

NATIONAL BESTSELLING AUTHOR
SANDRA KITT

Michaela Landry's quiet summer of
house-sitting takes a dramatic turn when
she finds a runaway teen and brings him
to the nearest hospital. There she meets
Cooper Smith Townsend, a local pastor
whose calm demeanor and dedication are
as attractive as his rugged good looks.
Now their biggest challenge will be to trust
that a passion neither planned for is strong
enough to overcome any obstacle.

Coming the first week of September 2008,
wherever books are sold.

ARABESQUE®

www.kimanipress.com   KPSKI040908

What Matters Most

ESSENCE BESTSELLING AUTHOR
GWYNNE FORSTER

Melanie Sparks's job at Dr. Jack Ferguson's clinic is an opportunity to make her dream of nursing a reality—but only if she can keep her mind off trying to seduce the dreamy doc. Jack's prominent family expects him to choose a wealthy wife. But he soon realizes he's fallen for the woman right in front of him…. Now he just has to convince Melanie of that.

*Coming the first week of October
wherever books are sold.*

ARABESQUE®

www.kimanipress.com